city of incident

Also by Annie Zaidi

Bread, Cement, Cactus: A Memoir of Belonging and Dislocation
Prelude to a Riot: A Novel
Gulab
Love Story #1 to 14
The Good Indian Girl
Known Turf: Bantering with Bandits and Other True Tales
Crush
3 Plays: Untitled 1; Jam; Name, Place, Animal, Thing

Books edited by Annie Zaidi
Unbound: 2,000 Years of Indian Women's Writing

city of incident

a novel in twelve parts

annie zaidi

ALEPH BOOK COMPANY
An independent publishing firm
promoted by *Rupa Publications India*

First published in India in 2022
by Aleph Book Company
7/16 Ansari Road, Daryaganj
New Delhi 110 002

Copyright © Annie Zaidi 2022

The author has asserted her moral rights.

This is a work of fiction. Names, characters, places and incidents are either the product of the author's imagination or are used fictitiously and any resemblance to any actual persons, living or dead, events or locales is entirely coincidental.

All rights reserved.

No part of this publication may be reproduced, transmitted, or stored in a retrieval system, in any form or by any means, without permission in writing from Aleph Book Company.

ISBN: 978-93-90652-12-9

1 3 5 7 9 10 8 6 4 2

For sale in the Indian subcontinent only.

Printed at Thomson Press India Ltd., Faridabad

This book is sold subject to the condition that it shall not, by way of trade or otherwise, be lent, resold, hired out, or otherwise circulated without the publisher's prior consent in any form of binding or cover other than that in which it is published.

For Annu mamoo, who opened the door to let me step into the biggest city of all.

And for beloved friends without whom all cities would be as ruins in a desert.

Contents

1. A Policeman Reflects on Accidents,
   Careless Women, and Infanticide   1
2. A Salesgirl Rides the Footboard,
   Forgetting the Price of Love   9
3. A Bank Teller Sees a Happy Baby
   on the Street, and Wants to Die   20
4. A Wood Worker Incites Desire in
   One Heart and Self-loathing in Another   33
5. A Housewife Walks Out with Her
   Children but Fails to Board the Train   41
6. A Beggar Recalls Babies in Plastic Bags
   and Makes Furtive Love   54

7. A Woman Encounters Love in Illicit Places,
   and Watches Over Her Lover's Wife   60

8. A Security Guard Reflects on Invisible
   Threats and the Betrayal of Friends   72

9. An Adulterous Man Revisits the Truth
   After His Lover Falls to Her Death   80

10. A Trinket Seller Accepts Treats from
    a Snake Charmer While Her Husband
    Languishes in Jail   90

11. A Man with a Dead Wife Comes
    Upon a Balloon Seller and a Baby   103

12. A Manager Picks Up Scraps of Other
    People's Lives, and Attempts to Restore
    Her Own   112

Acknowledgements   135

A Policeman Reflects on Accidents, Careless Women, and Infanticide

Between nine o'clock and midnight, this man rides in the first-class twenty-four-hour ladies' coach on the Western line.

Fourteen years in the railway police and he never thought of his uniform as any kind of armour but ever since he was deputed to guard duty in the ladies' coach, he feels that it is one. His rifle sits on the cushioned teal blue of the first-class seat, as if it has nothing to do with him. A plop of foam sticks out of the rexine seat cover. He notices that it matches the khaki of his uniform trousers. His fingers pick at the foam and he wonders if the ladies have been ripping up seat covers on purpose. No, he decides. It must be the urchins who clamber in off the tracks and ride ticketless. But if the ladies did want to rip up seat covers, what would they use? Knives?

They carry knives, some of them. He has seen them squatting on the train floor, chopping up beans and shelling peas into plastic bags while on their way home. It is more likely one of these ladies who carry a knife while travelling than an urchin who doesn't even have a bag to hide it in.

What else could a woman use? A hairpin, possibly. A thin, black metal hairpin. He had scratched his forearm against one such pin and had been startled

Annie Zaidi

at the sliver of blood it drew, for he hadn't noticed any sharp objects on the cluster of heads surrounding him. Or perhaps it was a needle. Those are quite sharp too and the ladies do knit and crochet in the train. Or a safety pin. Yes. That is just the sort of thing a lady might do if she was sitting by herself in an empty coach. Her restless fingers would take a safety pin to the teal-blue rexine. Stick it in. Gouge. Rip it up with a wrench and a twist of her wrist.

He settles into a deep groove in the seat created by the pressure of a heavy bottom. Day and night, hundreds of bottoms have vied for this particular seat. It is right under the fan and across from the doorway where someone is always standing, hugging the smooth metal pole. College girls, urchins, vendors of combs and plastic mobile phone covers. His own bottom fits snugly into the groove that's right under the fan. There was a time he dwelt upon the bottom that might have created such a groove. He had been assigned by the nation to shield this bottom from harm. Covered in nylon, polycot, denim, 100 per cent cotton, a blooming garden of colourful bottoms. Bottoms highlighted by silver and red embroidered patterns on the rear pockets of jeans. Bottoms raised up, quarrelsome or querulous.

The urge to stare has worn off now. These days he enters the first-class ladies' coach at Churchgate and kicks off his shoes, first thing. Then he peels off his socks and stuffs them into his trouser pockets. He puts his feet up on the empty seat across, takes the rifle off his shoulder, resting it on the seat beside him. For fifteen minutes he travels thus, as though he were one of them. Weary soul on his way home, staring out of the barred window at neatly stacked boxes of light. Up, up, up the ladder of night. Up, until they're scraping the cracked heels of the sky.

He almost believes it, that he is one of them. The spell breaks at ten minutes to eleven when the crowd swells and grows urgent, and he is overwhelmed, again, by kohl glances and thick perfumes. He takes his feet off the seat, slides them into his shoes, and keeps his eyes trained on the floor. Yellow soles with blue straps, red with golden heels, painted toes. Once all the seats have been filled, he picks up his rifle and moves towards the open doors of the train. The ladies shuffle, moving a few inches this way and that to make room for him.

He feels better once he is standing on the footboard, perched halfway between their world and his own. He stands his rifle upright, tucked between his left knee and the train door. Then he tunes the radio on his phone and plugs up his ears. The wind is in his hair now and the crackling radio in his blood.

This is the tender hour. Today a woman with a heavy northeastern accent has called in. She is asking Love Guru what to do about a boyfriend who refuses to accept that he is, indeed, her boyfriend. He spits *Saala!* into the wind and braces himself as the train thuds past the stink of Mahim creek. Love Guru lectures the girl a trifle too long. He switches to another station.

At this hour, all the radio jockeys get throaty and mellow, swaddling listeners with the innocence of the fifties and sixties. They play *Come into my arms, for this night may never return*, and his blood grows sluggish with maudlin sentiment. Clustered around him, purses and bags pinched under armpits, each of the ladies is wearing her own music. Heavy lids over thorn bush eyes. He is careful not to brush up against them.

A crochet lace of slum tenements runs along the track, single points of light serenading homecomers. Once, as the train slows down, he sees a man in a red vest bent over a kerosene stove, stirring a pot. The ash of night flies into his eyes. All their eyes. The trundle of wheels softens his ears. All their ears.

He nearly forgets his khaki uniform, his government

issue belt and shoes. He forgets he is only here to guard them against men. In his head, he lectures the ladies. *How careless you'll are! Why hang out here when the coach isn't even all that crowded? Is the breeze so very cool? Is it worth your life? And why did you cross the railway tracks? I saw you! Are you so weak that you cannot climb a flight of stairs? Why do you not wait until the train stops fully before you step off? Waitwaitwait!*

He thinks of telling them that shiny slippers and heels are not suited to this daily balancing act on the footboard of fast trains. One little slip. One could roll for several metres on the platform, crash into iron pillars and food stalls with sharp metallic edges. Ribs might crack upon impact. Do they know that one can lose one's hearing if one falls at an awkward angle? It sounds impossible but he knows a woman and that's just what happened to her. Fifty per cent deaf now. The accident didn't affect her jaw but, for several days, she seemed to have lost her voice too. The doctor said her whole body had gone into shock. Each organ would take its own time. Her eyes would take time to focus when he called out her name. Her tongue would not register sweet and bitter. She would not tell him that he was putting too much milk in the coffee, and to forget it, she'd just do it herself. One

Annie Zaidi

thoughtless move and nothing is the same.

So many accidents happen these days. But that word—accident—it belongs to the vocabulary of the innocent. For him, there are only incidents. Some incidents are followed by investigations, which are followed by pleadings, cautionings, offerings. A link-chain of unfolding incident. What was that old song? *This city is a city of incident.* Yes, that's just what it is.

He thinks of that old woman again. He is certain, even now, that she had done something, and right in front of his eyes. It was the first train of the morning and the commuters had turned off the harsh white tube lights inside the coach. Most of them were fisherfolk and flower vendors, heading out to the wholesale markets, nodding over their damp baskets. And there was that woman, her eyes like snarling beasts on the other side of the metal barriers separating first class from second.

She held something in her lap. An odd shape wrapped in black plastic, her fingers laced around it and a corner of her sari drawn over it. Did he imagine the plastic bag moving?

As their eyes met, he saw it: the flicker of an incident. She saw, too, his cop's gaze taking her in. Wisps of grey at her temples, thick nose, short neck.

She had unentangled her gaze, hitched her sari up higher at the waist as if she was getting busy in the kitchen, and moved towards the door. She stood on the footboard and, just as the station came into view, tossed the bag. A full-armed throw. A brief glance over her shoulder as the train pulled up to the platform, a defiant lunge before the wheels stopped turning.

She had disembarked at a little run and melted into the crowd. Brown sari, he recalls, the colour of chocolate, worn over a maroon petticoat, a middle-aged waist. Plastic slippers. Black hair coiled into an oily loop, a shiny buckle. She had no handbag. A tiny purse was probably tucked into her blouse. He remembers each detail and yet, he thinks now that if he passed her on the street, he would not recognize her.

A Salesgirl Rides the Footboard, Forgetting the Price of Love

This woman is so transparent, the evil eye cannot fall upon her. Perhaps the evil goes right through her body, falling on the person standing right behind her in queue for the renewal of a second-class pass.

Not that she travels second class. She travels first class, bindaas. Who can challenge her? She wears sleeveless tops and big dangly earrings, just like a college girl. She has an office job and a faux leather handbag with a Hello Kitty clasp that she polishes once a week with Brasso. Nobody would look at her and say that she doesn't look first class. Besides, in the terrible crush of the morning, no ticket examiner dares enter the compartment. No commuter could be expected to reach into her purse to extract a ticket or a pass. All arms are trapped, pressed, and pinned down by a dozen other arms and shoulders. All the ladies must suck in their bellies and squash each other's breasts as they make their way from seat to aisle to door. There is safety in such crowds.

Even so, she is aware that luck is on her side. Night after night, she travels in the first-class coach when it is near empty. In four years, not once has any ticket examiner shown up and asked to see her ticket. For this, she is grateful. Also, for the cop who is on duty in the ladies' compartment after nine o'clock. His khaki uniform made her nervous at first, she being a law-breaker of sorts. However, as the weeks went by, she decided that his presence was further evidence of her good luck. She feels safe, no matter how late she travels.

The best time to travel in this city is between 9.30 and 10.30 p.m. After that, it feels like rush hour all over again. At 11 p.m., gents are allowed to board the second-class ladies' coach, but the ladies refuse to be squashed into any coach with gents, tickets be damned. So they come pouring into the neighbouring coach, the first class, which is reserved for ladies all twenty-four hours. This is usually the family crowd, mothers with children in tow. Big noisy groups. These women know none of the unspoken rules of train etiquette—how to sit, how to stand, where to get off. If you snap at them, they expect sympathy. They expect you to give up your seat just because they're carting babies.

She makes it a point to turn her head away, smiling the barely-restrained smile of the long suffering. She has learnt how to do this from the first-class ladies. They rarely scream or shout when the irregulars invade the compartment. Instead, they exchange glances and roll their kohl-smudged eyes. They think they can tell who is, and isn't, first class at a glance. Tacky gold lace edging a sari. Lots of bracelets. Flashy red sindoor in the parting of their hair. Polyester burqas. Flushed faces, high-pitched voices and, above all, their easy excitability. It's a picnic for them, being out in a local train.

Some nights, a first-class pass-holder will lose her cool. She will snap at one of the second-class ladies, asking her to mind where she steps, pointing out that this is first class. Then some of the other ladies will chime in. *How much we tolerate, but these people take advantage of our silence. Now if only a ticket examiner would show up. The way we are suffering! We don't get to sit down even at eleven at night! What's the point of paying for a first-class pass? Pointless!*

Some nights, the ladies turn on the cop who is travelling with them, their indignant voices rising. *What's the use of having a policeman with us if he cannot enforce the law? Why doesn't he throw them out? They're not satisfied with getting into first class, now they want a seat too! All of us fools who pay for the first class, we stand here and look at their faces. Just look at them, they're sitting there grandly as if their father owns the railway.*

He can hear them, despite his earphones. She can

tell from the way he carefully keeps his face averted, the way he stares out into the dark night. He ignores their indignation, doesn't say a word. She likes this about him.

She knows he boards the train at Churchgate. She herself boards at that station and is careful not to look him in the eye as she enters the coach. She picks a seat so she can sit with her back turned to him. She kicks off her yellow slippers with their bright blue straps, puts up her feet on the empty seat across. Idly, she speculates on the shape of his wife. His moustache suggests a wife. His belly suggests a wife. What does she want with a man who has a wife waiting at home?

The crowd swells with each passing station and, at the third stop, she moves to another seat, angled so that she can observe him as he stands on the footboard. A pair of white earphones stick out from under his khaki collar. She wonders what songs he listens to. She can guess. It is the tender hour. All the radio jockeys get breathy and the songs get cloyingly sweet.

White earphones, sentimental songs. There is something to his posturing, the languor of his backside as he stands on the footboard, one knee bent, the wind in his hair, and his rifle standing in the corner. A wistful married man. Her fingers tingle when she thinks of running them through his hair. He must be, what, thirty-five? There might be children.

So? It's not like she wants his children. What for? She has had a child, though nobody would guess. She still looks like a college girl. What happened to her, it was bad luck. One of those rare times her luck turned against her. Some would say it was very bad luck. Girls live in terror of this very thing. But it happened and now her eyes are wide open. In a way, it was good for her. She learnt quickly what this world is. Men's ways.

Her own mother doesn't believe in luck. She says everything is a consequence of your own deeds. Action, reaction. A rock of a mother. Hard. Immoveable. Still, luck was on her side. Any other girl would have been thrown out of the house as soon as the family found out. Her life would be ruined, trying to bring up a baby with no college degree, no job, no room to live in, no family support. Her best years would have been wasted. But her own mother stood by her, kept her at home until the baby was born, then she managed things quietly. She had once tried to ask—how? where?—but her mother had given her a warning look. *I left it somewhere. Don't ask again.*

Somewhere means somewhere, a place where such

babies are left, she supposes. She doesn't want to know exactly where. She had not held it, not for a minute. The only glimpse she had of its face was over her mother's shoulder. A pale, scrunched-up face nestled against her mother's thick, short neck. Her mother's oily bun, black except for a few strands of white, shone against the little black head. Then they were both gone. Somewhere. Why think of 'where' now? It is more important to think about where she herself is headed.

She managed to get her senior secondary school certificate after the third attempt. Now she works at an office and this is a big step up. She will not work in other people's homes like her mother does. Office work is better, even if she just makes and serves tea three times a day, and dusts all the tables and chairs. She has to show up at least half an hour before the other staff, but this too is stroke of good luck. It means that she can board an early morning train, when the crush isn't so bad. Well, it is bad, but she can get into the train without worrying about being elbowed in her ribs and slipping off the footboard, or losing her grip on the door handle. If she waited to travel at eight in the morning, there would be too many hands on the handle and if she did manage to grab the metal pole in the doorway, she isn't sure of being able to haul her body into the compartment.

There are other advantages to getting in early. She cleans the office at her own pace and there's time to wash up properly later, to do up her eyes and lips in the washroom, where there's a full-length mirror. She hates being watched as she does the dusting. She likes to do the job slowly, turning on the overhead lights one at a time, so that the expanse of the office unfolds before her eyes as if it were her own private dawn. In the long half-lit room, she examines each desk critically. Photos of children in swimming pools. A souvenir postcard from Phuket. She has turned it around to see how much it costs to buy a postcard in Phuket. She knows that one of the managers has to eat a snack every two hours. There's a diet chart under his keyboard.

Later, after she's made and served the morning tea, she retreats. She has a chair to herself in the pantry and here, she flips through magazines for an hour. Her mother never had a chair to sit on in any of the dozen houses she worked in. Not one chair in thirty years. The best thing about this office job is that she meets a higher standard of person here. These people order lunch from restaurants every day. They discuss the relative merits of food courts at various shopping malls. Some of them drive to work in cars, even the women.

She listens to their chatter as she watches the milk come to a boil in the pantry. What's more, she derives a sweet pleasure from knowing that even these women, business managers who drive their own cars, are not rich enough to buy clothes at the shop where she works after office hours. No, not a shop. It's a store. She has been told that she must say 'store' every time she answers the phone or welcomes a customer. And they're not to be called 'customers'. She is to say 'our guests' and treat them as such. Offer a glass of water in a long-stemmed wine glass. Ask if they'd like some green tea while she wraps up their purchases.

She puts in four hours at the store on weekday evenings, eight hours on the weekend. She has learnt to call it 'the weekend' and not Saturday-Sunday. Twelve hours of work, plus four hours of commute. She still doesn't make as much money as her mother makes, cooking and cleaning in just two homes in town. She doesn't mind though. At the store, she has eaten an avocado, smashed and spread out on toast with a sprinkling of pepper. She has learnt to use a pepper mill. She is learning about clothes, how to tell first class from second class, how to cheat at class. Four months after she started out at the store, she critically examined herself and her wardrobe, and came to the conclusion that her jeans and fitted t-shirts marked her out as lower middle class. Just about. She changed the way she did her hair then, pulling it up into a high ponytail or using a pencil to wind it into a high bun. That way her cheekbones stood out. She stopped using liquid eye liner and instead learnt to smudge her kohl, as if she couldn't be bothered with neatness. She has begun to wear red or deep purple on her lips instead of the timid shades of brown her mother favours.

The store manager has begun to offer her some of her own cast-offs. She has put them away carefully, wrapped in the same tissue paper she uses for the store's customers. Guests, not customers. Before she can start wearing those clothes, she will need to fill out a bit. She intends to. Not too much, just five kilos. She's seen the diet chart and she knows how to do it. She's going to eat all the avocados she can find, drink all the milk that can be spared in the office pantry.

Next quarter, she is going to buy herself a first-class pass. Then she will stand on the footboard of the train and hug the metal pole before anyone else gets to it. One of these nights, she will catch this railway policeman's eye, and she will ask him an ordinary question. Something about the radio, maybe. Or about some railway incident. Like the time she saw a crazy woman sliding under the wheels of a train, hiding there, waiting for the train to start moving.

Waiting to be cut up into bits. Nice clothes and all. Middle class, not one of these homeless mad ones. It didn't happen though. They spotted her. She was dragged out in the nick of time. By God! She got such a thrashing from the public. The public thrashing a woman, imagine! Have you ever seen anything like that?

She might laugh then, make a wry comment about the city. *This city will forgive anything and anyone, except for those who delay the trains.*

She just needs to get some words going. She wants to get something going. In the meantime, she will maintain her looks. She drinks the juice of carrots and sweet limes. She has learnt to say, 'No sugar' when she places her order. Luckily, there is a juice stall right on the platform where she waits to board the first-class ladies' coach. With her smile, the brassoed clasp on her handbag, her green eyes, and a bit of luck, she'll go places.

A Bank Teller Sees a Happy Baby on the Street, and Wants to Die

This woman wears a string of jasmine in her hair, all the six days that she goes to work at the bank. The secret joke among the staff at her branch is that the sweetness of the scent and brilliance of the flowers in her hair stand in inverse proportion to the sourness of her tongue and the blackness of her mood.

It is not such a secret joke really. Well, they can say what they want. There is cause enough for her black moods. She has the worst luck. Not a day passes when something doesn't go wrong. People walk right into her on the street, on the skywalk, on railway platforms. Someone will step on her toes on the day she decides to wear open-toed sandals. On a day that she has to wait at the bus stop for a few minutes, there will be a dead rat lying there. Four crows will descend and proceed to rip apart its skin, pecking away at its flesh, and even the arrival of the bus will not cause them to flap their wings and fly away. They will simply hop a few inches towards safety and wait, beady eyed, beaks busy with scraps of red flesh. She will be forced to walk around the crows and the corpse of the dead rat and then she will miss her bus. This will happen to her a week after her father dies and she will remember what the priest who came home for the last rites had told her, that the souls of departed ancestors always return home, often as birds. That's the kind of luck she has had.

There is always someone ahead of her at the ticket counter even though she lines up to purchase a first-class pass. What are the chances that will happen to someone every single time? Yet, it happens to her. She has never, not once in her thirty-three years, been the first person in a queue. On a hot day, if she finds herself alone in an empty train compartment and finds a seat right under the fan, that will be the day the fan will not function. The city's grit chooses to fly straight into her eyes every time there's a bit of breeze.

Luck has been against her from the start. She was born in the wrong country to start with. Then, of all cities, it had to be this one. Crowds and noise. If there is something she hates, it is crowds and noise. Nothing has ever gone the way her heart willed it.

She curses her luck unfairly though. Consider her body. Heavy breasts, round hips, slender waist, arms toned from hanging onto overhead bars in buses and trains. Many women would call it good luck, but not she. She can think only of her body's failure, although this is the one thing she does not complain about publicly. Out loud, she complains about rats and buses and customers who need to be told four

Annie Zaidi

times to take the token and wait their turn instead of surrounding the teller's desk and waving withdrawal slips in her face.

Stamping, signing, counting. She can't stand another day of it and yet she can't give it up. Her husband has never said that she could quit. He has a government job, pension, insurance. Yet, she must work until the children come. They will need the savings when he retires, he says. He doesn't own a house, after all, and he doesn't do much under the table. She has worked eleven years now and there are no children to justify her quitting. Her husband says she will get bored without a job. *Why do you want to sit alone at home? For what, to stare at the four walls?*

Despite her job, she has time to stare at the four walls and the ceiling too. He's been on the night shift for a while now. All of last week, he entered the house past two in the night, smelling of damp socks, chicken curry, and lemon. No need to wake up just to warm up his dinner, he said. He was not awake at breakfast and she was never home for lunch. On his weekly day off, when at last they ate a meal together, she asked what they should do in the evening, and he shrugged. *What's there to do?*

A woman always knows her own peril, her mother

used to say. She saw it clearly then: her hair had gone from a lush, loose knot at the nape of her neck to a tight knot sticking out at the back of her head like a black ping-pong ball. Her shirts were loose enough to merely suggest shape rather than assert it. Her mother was right. She does know.

Knowledge is power. She dimly recalls one of her classmates saying it with a balled-up fist, swaying left to right, right to left, as if all power was indeed concentrated in her own pink palm, as if she would grasp the whole assembly thus—the school with all its teachers and students and cleaning staff. She faces the knowledge of her peril and her tart luck with balled-up fists and nails clipped short.

Going up the railway bridge, she has watched women of all shape and colour carrying infants. She has seen them smacking toddlers who cannot climb the stairs fast enough. She has seen pregnant women heaving into first class, eyes darting about for an empty seat, then looking hopefully at those who have managed to snag one. She refuses to meet their eyes. Let them quit their jobs if they cannot handle the commute. Let them sit at home and stare at the four bloody walls. They don't mind panting and sweating with a man on top, do they? Let their backs ache for a few months now. She doesn't turn her head even when she has heard somebody cry out, *She's fainting, this one! She's going to faint!*

Then comes a day when she sees a man asleep under the elevated railway, his lean arm wrapped around a baby, and the sight makes her feel faint.

She has left the bank early on this day, for no good reason. It was just that she could picture herself sitting at home, doing nothing at all, so she told the manager that she had a doctor's appointment. She knows there will be whispered speculation the moment she leaves the room. *No children, no? Not too old, is she? What sort of doctor, did she say?*

She doesn't care. She is determined to go home and just stare at the four walls today. In keeping with her luck, the bus is overflowing even though it is the middle of the afternoon. The seats reserved for ladies are all taken so she stands, knees resisting the lurch of each braking motion. She almost makes it to her stop without incident but then, at a red light, she sees him from the bus window: a man asleep under the elevated rail bridge. Brown, bare arms and a mud-yellow sleeveless vest pulled up to his chest, showing a shining bronze coin of a nipple. A dust-covered baby, its naked bottom pressed against the man's belly.

A black whorl seems to grow behind her eyes. She has to ask someone to allow her to sit down. Someone forces her to accept a piece of candy. She puts it in her mouth, rests her head on someone's shoulder. Whose? Someone asks if she is pregnant. An old woman. She finds herself nodding. Someone else pats her shoulder. Her eyes remain fixed upon the man and the baby asleep in the dust until the signal changes and the bus lurches forward.

She gets off at the next stop. It is not her stop but she cannot bear to go home now. She thinks it will do her good to walk a little. Soon she is back at the spot where the man is lying on his side. His eyes are open and she sees that he is staring at a girl across the road, the one selling beads. The baby, wearing only an oversized shirt with all its buttons missing, is fast asleep. His baby roundness and softness remain intact, despite the heat and the hunger that have turned his hair to straw.

It is not his child, she tells herself. Their faces are not alike. She feels compelled to say it aloud. *Where did you get this child?*

The man disentangles his gaze from the bead-necklace girl. Slowly he sits up and takes in this woman. Her face, hair, sandals. His way of looking at her is different from the way he was looking at the bead-necklace girl. He looks at her as he might look at a black bull pawing the ground. *He's ours*, he says at last.

Her eyes do not leave the child's body. *Yours? Yours and whose? Hers?*

She points at the bead-necklace girl across the road, tipping her forefinger with a contempt she does not actually feel. Her voice is too loud. The girl has turned around and is staring back at her. At her pointing finger.

The man begins to laugh. A moment later, the bead-necklace girl also cracks a smile although she is too far away to have heard anything. As if this were all a joke. As if this woman radiated a kind of clownishness that was self-evident.

My husband is in the police, she blurts out. *I could get you locked up.*

The man's crinkled eyes grow still now. The laughter recedes from his face. He sits there, one hand resting on the baby's thigh, his black eyes staring back at her. There is no doubt that he believes her. She could get him locked up if she wanted to.

She wants to say something else. Is this any way to bring up a child—naked in the dust? If a man sleeps all day, what does he hope to earn? Do they nap together like this every afternoon? But now his eyes are locked onto hers and her mouth has suddenly gone dry.

She spits out the remnant of the candy into the dust and walks away from him. Her gait is resolute even though she has no idea where she is headed. Not home, not to stare at the four walls. Not to the bank. Where should she go? There is not one house open to her in this city crawling with tens of millions.

Her feet pause outside a restaurant called Sunny's. She has eaten here before, during her college days, and she knows it will be dingy inside. There will be a mouldy picture of the restaurant owner's father on the wall with a dusty garland of sandalwood shavings strung around the frame. Each table will sustain the wilting bodies of men who do not have a fixed lunch hour. Shopkeepers, electricians, home tuition teachers. She can already see the shape of their curving backs, their eyes lowered to their plates, fingertips dyed yellow with the turmeric in their curried chicken. She is certain that if she decides to step in, the waiters will be rude and the food greasy. She knows why. It is her blighted luck. After she has eaten there, she'll be burping up stale curry all night.

She lets her feet decide and they coax her onto

a familiar route. Back to the bus stop, and the bus takes her back to the railway station. She goes down onto the platform and stands clustered with other women. She boards the first-class ladies' and is jostled, pushed. She cannot get a seat. Why would she find an empty seat? Nothing in life comes easy. Life is a series of skirmishes, misadventures, disappointments. That's what her Guruji used to say. *Learn to accept disappointment.*

Whenever she visited his ashram, those were the words he would offer her. *First, learn to accept disappointment.* Up on the wall, in large curling letters, he had got his philosophy painted in tasteful silver and white. *The universe owes you nothing.*

Her father held a similar philosophy though he put a jollier face on it. *Life is a merry-go-round at the fun fair*, he used to say. *Once you're on it, you're on it. You can't make it stop nor can you force it to change speed; just enjoy the ride.*

It occurs to her now that although she can't make the merry-go-round stop, she can jump off the ride. There is a tremulousness in her wrists, a needle of pain tunnelling through her forehead. She goes to the train door and wraps her arms around the smooth metal pole. She listens to the khad-khadaak khad-khadaak music of the wheels. Her dupatta catches the wind and snaps outwards, flying outside the compartment.

The train is fast enough but she is afraid. She might lose a hand or a leg and survive. With her luck? No, she can't take the chance. She decides to wait until the train chugs into the last station, holding her stance all the while, embracing the warm pole. The hordes waiting on the platform are cruel, unstoppable. The ladies don't wait for the train to stop before they dive in. Dainty slippers slip and slither on the metal floor; elbows and knees smash against each other. They will mow down whoever stands in their way and, today, she is in their way. They cannot grab the pole so they reach for her body and use it to heave themselves into the compartment. Some of the women scream incoherencies as they rush to grab empty seats. One woman punches her in passing, curses her, calls her a cunt.

She keeps her cheek pressed to the warm metal, eyes squeezed shut. She waits until all the women have squeezed past, settled down wherever they found room, then steps off the footboard and starts walking the length of the platform. Slowly, as if she were taking a leisurely stroll. A man bumps into her and says as much. *What? Is this a garden?*

Annie Zaidi

She stops where the platform ends and glances up at the digital indicator. Two minutes to departure. She jumps down to the track, bends double, crouches under the wheels nearest the engine end of the train. Her head is tucked between her knees. She can hear the announcer, beseeching passengers to keep the station and its surroundings clean, to throw rubbish in the rubbish bins and not to spit because spit leads to the spread of disease, not to travel on the footboard, for it is dangerous, and to report any unattended or suspicious object to the railway police. One minute to departure. She hears the hoarse, familiar cry of the man who sells dry bhel-puri in twists of paper torn out from glossy magazines. A pouff of the engine. A whistle. Ten seconds before the wheels start to turn. Then, rough hands on her arms, the snap of her wrist, blows around her ears.

Later, she senses the passing impatience of feet that have to slow down to walk a curve around her body. Thousands of feet. Crowds and noise. She can see them but she cannot hear what they said. They are probably cursing her. Cunt. Stupid. Stupid cunt.

Funny, how distant everything seems to be when you cannot hear things, she thinks. It is as if she weren't here, a heap dragged and dumped onto the platform. It is as if she were instead examining a faded photograph of herself curled up on the platform. As if, from the safe refuge of the future, she was watching a train pull away.

A Wood Worker Incites Desire in One Heart and Self-loathing in Another

This man is the one being shaken awake by a baby. For makers of bamboo huts and mats, trappers of slow birds, men with languorous bones and songs in languages nobody else in the city understands, there is no real work to be found.

He has drawn the heavy June day over his limbs and fallen asleep on bare earth, under the new elevated rail. There is no garden here although a battered sign further down the road says that this garden is maintained by one private limited company. He doesn't know this company or what it does, but he has had a brush with one of these big private limited companies back home, in his village. His mother had taught him to weave bamboo mats so he could make his own hut before he got married, and also to make a living in the lean season. Walls, roof, bed, stool—nothing he can't do with bamboo. It is a great thing, his mother used to say, jiggling his baby sister on her scrawny thighs, to be independent. *Freedom!* That was the meaning of manhood. To be able to make your own hut with your own hands. But for all his skill, when it was time, there was nowhere to put up his hut. All the land was taken away by the private limited company. They didn't even come to ask if they could buy the land. Everything was settled between the government and the company. There was no time to salvage anything when the bulldozers came with the police. Now here he is, sleeping under the elevated railway bridge on a June afternoon. Nothing he can't do with his hands, but nothing he can do either.

He lies on a patch of earth where no grass will take hold. Young palm trees, transplanted a month ago to beautify the underside of the elevated rail, have died from the bilious traffic fumes. Between two palms, this man has fallen asleep and a baby is now squatting beside him, patting his legs, patting his belly. Patting his face.

From a distance, onlookers cannot tell whether the man is asleep or dead. A few yards off to the left, there is a colourful clump of plastic bags. The city's fingers unfurl and let loose a stream of bags filled with the remains of puffed rice and Kurkure wrappers. The undersides of bridges and the elevated rail serve as dustbin and spittoon. Those who live here do not scream. Perhaps they too have been let loose at this spot by the unseeing fingers of time. As if they were as light as plastic bags, the government moves them around as easily, with as little fuss.

Up crawls the baby. Pat-patting the man's belly, chest, face. It is not the sleep of the dead, after all.

The man's head is raised. A hand is raised. Those who watch, hold their breaths. The baby leans forward, its bare bottom turned to the traffic. The man's hand is not raised, after all. It is merely extended. One lean arm curls around the baby's shoulders. The baby lies down, pressing his back against the man's bare chest and is asleep before the traffic light can change.

The man falls down the shaft of afternoon. The mound of plastic does not stir. The traffic light turns green. A woman wearing a midnight-blue top with a white collar is trapped behind a slow-moving bus. She bangs her fist on the horn but before she can get across the signal, the light has turned yellow, then red again. A white plastic bag floats free of the fingers of the gainfully employed, snags on one of the transplanted palm trees. Not a leaf stirs this afternoon.

The stalled traffic watches the man and the baby. What sort of man will the baby grow into? A man with pat-pat-patting hands. A hugged man. A woman watches him, feeling bloated with unshed tears. Her spine grows warm with false memory. She has never slept on bare earth. Her own childhood was spent in high-rises. The only change in her life has been that she moved from her parent's two-bedroom apartment to the two-bedroom apartment rented by her husband.

Annie Zaidi

Now here she is, trapped behind the wheel, obsessively adjusting the air-conditioning, as she watches a man under a bridge with a sleeping baby.

The man has drifted into wakefulness. His head is turned and his gaze transfixed upon another woman who is standing across the road with a load of jewellery. She wears the neat, flat-pleated skirt of her tribe. The hem of the skirt is clean, not yet ragged. That, the silver belt around her taut waist, and a pleasant self-assurance of eye and jaw betrays her. It speaks of recent arrival in the city.

There's a twitch in his calf muscles, an itch on the soles of his feet. He wonders from where and with whom she has come into the city. Where does she sleep at night? Does she know that men like him doze off during the day but that they sleep very little at night, that they keep watch over their families? He could tell her that he knows how to build a house, how to trap pheasant and quail. Not that he's seen any birds other than crows here. He watches her cross the road with her load of metal and bead necklaces and bracelets. Row upon row upon row of trinkets strung on a bamboo frame. It must add up to ten kilos, maybe fifteen. She must be a strong girl, like his sister who lifts bricks all day at a construction site.

Not like the women who live inside the tall buildings on either side of the elevated rail. He has seen these women, even spoken to a few. His mother had tried to sell handwoven mats and baskets when they had first arrived in the city. These building women grunted as they bent to pick up things. Blubbery bellies and swollen ankles even before their hair had turned white. Some of them would not bend at all. He had to pick up the basket they fancied and hold it up for scrutiny. He studied their faces, their sharp features dissolved by fat. The round circles of their eyes spinning with suspicion as they stood over him, shifting their weight from one thick ankle to the other, they compared two baskets of the same size, searching for some hidden clue as to which one had greater merit.

Unbidden, that other foot returns to mind. A bony ankle with toenails painted red. A whole arm, with some of the glass bangles still intact. It was a well-used arm, used to hard work, he had noted. He had been tasked with picking it up, putting together all the bits he could find. The torso, thankfully, was still attached to the head and had stopped bleeding by the time he got there. Two heads.

He had been confused by the two heads. Nearly the same size, except that the back of one had broken on impact and the mess inside had splatted out onto the railway track. He had baulked, not at the mess as much as at the sight of two heads and one torso. It was like something out of one of those childhood stories his mother used to tell. Six-armed gods and ten-headed demons. He tried to remember if she had told any stories about a deity with two heads but couldn't think of any.

He'd got yelled at for dawdling that day. The railway policeman standing above, on the edge of the platform, had shouted at him. *What are you gawking at? Is this some kind of circus? Is it the cinema? Hurry the fuck up, fucker. The line's been blocked for hours.*

When he stepped closer to the heads, he saw how it was. One of the arms, the one still attached to the torso, was wrapped tight around an infant. The second head belonged to the baby. It was funny how small the woman's head was, it was almost the head of the child. A small woman. Neat. A middle parting in her hair and a long line of bright orange sindoor in it. Her other hand must have been holding the hand of a bigger child. That one was all in bits. Glass from her shattered bangles shone on the track, bits of gold paint flecking green glass.

The shouting was constant that day. *Heyheyhey!*

Don't put it here. Not on the platform, you fucking idiot! What do you want, a sheet? Where's that fucker with the stretcher? Go ask the station master for a bedsheet.

He has tried, for months now, to shake loose that day from its quiet hold in his head but on such empty afternoons, days when he cannot find any work, it returns. The slight shudder of the rail overhead, the glint of sun on its metal, and his reluctant hands over the torso, the two heads, the three silver toe rings.

A dozen thoughts stream across his head. Motes of dust in a shaft of light. One of these thoughts is that things are always happening to people in this city. Every day, inside every head, there are tiny daggers scraping away. Turning, turning the soil of their minds until at last a bad idea turns up. Then something happens, as surely as the night must fall. And therefore, he wonders, how much longer before something bad happens to him?

Annie Zaidi

A Housewife Walks Out with her Children but Fails to Board the Train

The first train serves as an alarm clock for this woman. Between 5.32 and 5.36 a.m., the train silently trundles down the gleaming tracks that run perpendicular to the building she lives in.

When the ghud-ghuddup-ghud-ghuddup of the wheels slides out of earshot, she opens her eyes. Before her eyes are properly open, the soles of her feet have started twitching with the memory of four hundred paces. When she first arrived in the city, wearing one of the four cotton saris in her trousseau, she had counted her paces. Just for the sake of having something to occupy her mind. She has always counted things. Once she had spent the morning snack break counting the number of bricks the mason added every day to the new boundary wall that was coming up behind her school. The number of cycles at the cycle stand outside the cinema where she was not allowed to go with her friends but where her father would take the family twice a year. The number of saris and slippers packed into her red bridal suitcase.

In the train, on their way here, she counted all the pieces of luggage, over and over. Her husband and father-in-law, four new mattresses, a metal trunk, and four suitcases went into the luggage compartment. She was in the ladies' compartment with her mother-in-law, both clutching purses with all their gold jewellery inside. That was all they had been asked to carry, aside from a cloth bag full of snacks to last them a week. On her lap was the family's lunch, packed into two cardboard boxes.

They had moved to the new place with just their clothes and jewellery. Her husband had decided to sell everything else, including the four-poster bed her parents had sent as part of her dowry. He spoke of wanting to bring only new things into the new place. His own house, after all. New things could be made to fit its dimensions, new things that would last forever. Like this new relationship. Things like that were said in the beginning.

She had said nothing in response. Her heart thumped day and night as familiar things slipped out of her grasp. She had a new family, new clothes, new jewellery, new shoes, new bras and panties, new bus routes, new four-poster bed. Then, two months later, a whole new city and an apartment so new, there were no nails on the walls yet. No bed.

In this city, there were no cycle rickshaws and no tongas. Trains snuffled down its length like the fat-flecked blood in her mother-in-law's arteries. *It's an easy city*, her husband had assured her. *Step out of the building and there's the train station right there. Throw a pebble and you can hit it, it's that close.*

The cloth strap of the food bag had weighed down her left shoulder, and her mother-in-law's hand had pressed down on her right shoulder as they got off the train and waited for their husbands to emerge from the luggage compartment. Her husband had pointed out the new apartment. You could actually see it from the railway station platform. It was the tallest building east of the railway tracks, fourth window up, no balconies. Black metal grilles enclosed all the windows.

The luggage and her parents-in-law were loaded into two separate autorickshaws. Her husband had decided that they themselves would walk. *It's right here, and it will be good for you to know your way around on foot.* She had followed him, eyes to the ground, head and shoulders covered with her aanchal, stiff with its new starch. Four hundred paces, she had counted.

She has been to the railway station several times since and is no longer so timid. Fruits and vegetables are cheaper outside the railway station than at the shops nearer home. She now lifts her eyes and looks about. She sees women sitting with baskets of fruit, and women winding fresh jasmine into strands that men buy, folded up in waxy green leaves, tied up with white string, to take home, to other women. She sees jasmine coiled around oiled buns. She has never bought a strand for herself. It has never been bought for her either.

She buys jamuns, the plumpest, purplest ones, feeling the berries to test for ripeness. Palm fruit too, though she will not pick up the ones that have already been peeled and have been sitting exposed to the sun and dust for who knows how long. Instead, she stands over the old woman, watching her use a little knife, slender as the nail on her little finger, to unsheathe their slippery translucence. She thinks about sliding this translucent heart into her mouth, eating it whole in the middle of all this bustle with a hundred elbows knocking against hers, but she never does it.

There are days when she can cover the distance in three hundred and seventy paces. When she was pregnant, though, the road had stretched out to five hundred paces. She wonders how many steps it would be if she ran instead. The last time she ran, she must have been in the eighth standard. After the eighth, all extra-curricular and co-curricular activities in school were stopped. No painting, dancing, running, jumping, nothing, until the board exams were over. It was time to get serious, they said. Good and serious.

That she always had been. Even on her first day of school, she had not cried. She remembers the day. A blue uniform tunic and a canvas belt with three stripes. Blue, red, grey. She was just two and a half, but her mother had lied to the school principal, saying, she's three years old, just small for her age. Her mother still boasts about how she did not howl like all the other kids. She was told not to cry and she didn't.

Her mother likes telling stories about her. The time when she split open her knee and went all by herself to the dispensary. The time when she got her first pair of white ballerina shoes and was told to be careful not to dirty them, and how she became so cautious that she outgrew them before she had ever had a chance to wear them outside the house. The other thing her mother likes to say is, don't get too caught up with thinking. She said it when her wedding was arranged with her cousin's brother-in-law and she hadn't quite finished college. *Don't think so much. The only choice one has is how to do the thing that's got to be done. Do it easy and quick, it gets done easy and quick.*

That's how she does things, quick and quiet. They like her for it. They say how quiet and quick she is. When her first son arrived, they bought her a pair of gold jhumkas. Bracelets, the second time around.

Glistening black eyes, fat with pride and relief, now watch her move around the house, on her feet all day, doing what's got to be done: 6 a.m., tea for the in-laws, 6.30, tea for the husband. Start chopping potatoes for the breakfast poha at 6.45. Bathe and dress the older one at 7.15, feed him at 7.30. Walk him to the bus stop at 7.50. Call the others to breakfast at 8.30. Feed the younger one before eating herself. Take stock of the kitchen at 10. Start cooking lunch at 10.30.

Unknown to them, after the school bus has taken away her first child, she stops for a secret glug of time. Buses are rolling up and away. Red city buses. Yellow school buses. Blue mini-buses. There is one big white bus with a bluish-grey stripe running along its bottom that's always parked about a hundred paces from her building. Nobody calls out a destination, nothing is painted on its sides. Where does this bus go? Always parked at the same spot. Does it never move?

Between 7.45 and 8 a.m., she dallies, chewing her morsel of time like her mother chewed tobacco with a lick of lime stolen from the inside pocket of her father's jacket. She doesn't dare stay longer than ten minutes. The other mothers would have returned to the building and her family will start to wonder. Still, she stretches out the minute as far as it will go.

Standing at the bus stop, she counts. One two three four. Hundred one two three four. Two hundred one two three four.

She can do it in less than ten minutes. Four hundred paces. Or maybe it goes faster in her head. Maybe she will get tired after the first hundred. Still. Nobody would miss her for fifteen minutes. Even twenty. They'll miss her when breakfast is late. There's a train every two or three minutes, even though it is very crowded at eight in the morning. That is no time to be getting into a local train.

As she walks back to the building, her head is filled with a black square. It is the square that had stared back at her as she stood in the open doorway of a train painted two different shades of lilac. A clean black square of night had locked eyes with her across the railway tracks. Harsh white light from the platform was bouncing off the metal of the hand grips, the pole in the doorway, the tracks below. Silent, like a ghost ship, the train on the opposite platform chugged into the railway yard. As it pulled away, it seemed to her as if the black square of night was twisting around to look at her, as if a crooked finger had beckoned.

She had grown aware then, that she herself was framed in a black square such as the one she saw across

Annie Zaidi

the tracks. She, standing alone in the open doorway of a slow train, hugging the slippery metal pole with her whole body. A pause, a jerk. Engines pulling away in opposite directions. Then the night had swallowed it all up—platform, station, plastic-roofed shanties, the whole train.

It was three years ago, but the disco flash of the light bouncing off railway tracks still hangs in the corners of her eyes. She has never been out alone at night, before or since. That night, they had all gone to the beach. Her cousin's family was visiting. The sea was always refreshing and the food at the stalls was familiar and cheap, and her husband never lost his smile. But they had lingered too long. Her cousin wanted to play cards on the beach and her father-in-law couldn't stop a game once he started. Later, they had to run to catch the last train home. At the station, they had urged her to run, hurry, catch up. Each one had called out to her in turn. *Mummy, run! Run, Didi! Run, Bahu! Run!*

Her slippers slap-slapped clumsily and nearly came off her feet, but she had managed to clamber into the very last coach. She had no purse, no ticket, nothing but the thin nylon sari on her body. Her hair had come undone and the thudding in her chest was louder than the railway announcer's voice. Injunctions against travelling on the footboard of the train. The compartment was empty but she had not taken a seat. She stood in the doorway with the cold metal pole pressed against her body. Perfect black squares of night on the other side of her. Staring at her. Unreserved. Beckoning.

They had scolded her afterwards, for getting separated from the group. *What if she missed the train? It was the last train, didn't she know?* The scolding was no more than a cold wave sniping at her toes on the beach. She danced away from it easily, nimbly and, when she went to sleep that night, it was as if a cool black square were stretched across the length of her eyelids.

Four hundred paces. In bed, she imagines a black square spread out on either side of her. Night and its giant appetite. The black night framing her as she stood on the footboard. Smooth metal pole, her sentinel. Wind in her hair, undone.

They go out twice or thrice a year, visiting relatives on festivals. She has nobody else to visit. Once she had asked her husband if she could go visit her best friend from school. He had not looked up as he asked, *Why?* He may have read protest in her silence, for he asked the next day if she really wanted to go. She had shrugged as if it did not matter very much. He asked more questions. *Which friend was this? Was she married? How far was the place? How did she intend to travel? Could she leave the children for that long?*

He must have felt a pang of remorse later. He bought her a new sari that week. Semi-silk, a pattern of geometric designs in orange, blue, and green, with a line of gold thread along the edge. It was fancy, the sort of thing women wore on days like the inauguration of a new gadgets showroom or to an office party. He'd seen women in his office wearing such things to work the day before or after Diwali.

He watched her as she ran the back of her hand over the fabric and congratulated himself. She must be bored of the heavy silks she wore to festivals and weddings. This was lightweight, modern. She could wear it when she went out with him next. He would take her and the kids. Just them, not his parents. He teased her, then. *Don't save it too long, hmm? Not like the white shoes.* The whole thing was forgotten by Monday when routine came down on his six-hundred-and-fifty-square-foot world as surely as the pelting rain would come down in July.

She says nothing to him of the tightness in her

chest. A coiled snake of thought that doesn't go anywhere. It makes no sound. It gives her no words that she might blurt out. It sits there, quiet, cautious, watching her heart do its routine beat. Lately, she has begun to disappear into the bathroom for long minutes. Locking herself in, she stretches her arms as wide as they will go. She breathes out hard through her mouth, trying to dislodge the thing coiled around her heart. Like an old horse, she pants, her palms pressed against the pink bathroom tiles. The snake breathes slower too, so as not to waste its energy. It is saving its strength.

In her head, she counts the number of places she can think to go to, alone, just for one day. The answer is always zero. Her husband had asked the right question. How long can she leave the children, after all? If she took the children, how many steps could they walk before they got tired and began to cry? How much money did she have in her purse, and how many meals and train tickets would it buy?

Lately she has begun to offer water, not to the gentle rising sun but to the afternoon blaze. After lunch is cooked and while her second one is taking a nap, she goes up to the terrace with a brass dish and a pot of water. She piles her hair high on top of her head and offers the back of her neck to the white-hot sky, extending her arms forward and tipping water out of the pot. It splashes the hem of her sari, licks her bare feet. She is silent, not knowing the words that must accompany the ritual.

She keeps it up even in June although her mother-in-law has said it is not necessary. *The sun god does not expect devotion at such an hour.* Still, she dares not stop her daughter-in-law. Disapproval must take the guise of a begrudging approval in matters of prayer and ritual. Out the door and up the stairs she goes every day. Sun-like, she turns slowly, on her heel. Satellite-like, she perambulates the terrace. Terrace, flat, bus stop, flat, market, flat. Her path in the cosmos is fixed and the smallest deviation means to risk flying out of orbit.

The sun sends rivulets down her forehead, eyes. It gathers between her lips and chin, glints in the pool of water she has made on the concrete roof, and offers her face back to her. Tilting her head, she feels the tightness in her chest loosen. It is like the opening of a fist. A flash goes off behind her closed lids, an echo of something shiny and nourishing in its absolute blackness. White light bouncing off metal. Moonlight glinting on rail tracks.

A Beggar Recalls Babies in Plastic Bags and Makes Furtive Love

This man is spotted, face down, on the skywalk between 12.50 and 1.20 a.m. A grey-blue chequered blanket covers him, from his neck down to his ankles.

They can see him moving under the blanket, up-down, up-down. A matted shock of hair and the soles of feet so filthy, it is almost as if he has brown socks on. The last train on the Western line is pulling away, far below. The gaggle of women in click-clack heels and chiffon dresses and floppy bags in silver or gold sequins don't tarry on the bridge. He knows that they will feel wronged although he has not touched them, not even glanced at them. It is only when they are clattering down the endless staircase that they will start to mutter about how much they spend on quarterly commuter passes. *First class? Huh! Some people do not buy even second-class passes. By God, some people are living the high life rent-free! And on whose money? The skywalk was built with our taxes, no?*

During daylight hours, they may have dropped coins into his bowl. Perhaps they have seen his big eyes and one extended palm. Or perhaps he has no eyes. Or no palm. They call to mind the faces of the regulars—legless, armless, eyeless—who occupy the stairway leading up to the railway bridge. But they cannot link those stitched up faces, those stumps emerging from twisted shoulders and humped backs, with this man, a dark huddle under a blanket, moving up-down, up-down so urgently.

They walk fast across the bridge, as if he might jump up and lunge at one of them. In their haste to get away and their embarrassment, they cannot determine whether the person under him was a woman. They think of women because they do not want to think of girls. Not of the teenaged girl who hangs around at the station in the morning, a steel safety pin holding together the buttonless sides of her shirt, one teat exposed for the newborn slung across her waist in the makeshift harness of a pink nylon scarf.

The man, meanwhile, pauses to listen to their click-clack footsteps melding into the faint hum of cars on the street below. He knows they are in a hurry to get away from him. As for him, he is in no hurry. He lacks the hurry gene.

There used to be a woman at the station, a long time ago. She sat near the ticket counter and sold love apples, a foot-high pyramid laid upon a bed of waxy green leaves. She used to tell him that he must have been conceived in great fursat—on a languid moonless night, perhaps during the monsoon months. She remarked on how unhurried he was. Speech, gesture, work, gaze. He never retorted, never said that the alleged leisure of his conception had only hastened the speed at which he had been dumped after birth. Abandoned on top of a pile of unsorted rubbish. It used to haunt him. When he was a boy, his birth and abandonment occupied his mind constantly, but now he is grey and has seen many more garbage dumps and many other children abandoned there. Now he likes to say that he was born free. *Free!* At least he was not wrapped in a black plastic bag knotted tight so that he would choke to death before being discovered by some ragpicker like himself. At least, his mother gave him a chance to live. Who knows? Maybe she had even wanted him to live.

His own hands have undone the double knot on a black plastic bag. Whoever dumped it had thought to make it a double knot, to make sure its contents didn't spill out. His fingers had worked at the knots patiently although he had guessed what was in the bag.

One never knows these days. They keep saying do not touch any unattended objects. They run announcements at the station. A railway cop warned him once, never to touch bags he found lying around in empty coaches. But, of course, he opens all the bags he finds. He had felt the black bag from the outside. Felt its particular softness and firmness. It was not the sludgy softness of rotting food. Not a roll of fabric either. Nor the hardness of wood. Nor the bristle of fur. He guessed then and yet, he did not want to rip open the plastic. It was too still for it to matter and so, patiently, his fingers had prised open that double knot.

He is mystified by his own patience sometimes. He should hurry up right now, for instance. Railway cops carrying batons and rifles will be hopping off the trains now. They don't usually take the bridge but what if they did tonight? A hundred things happen that are not supposed to happen. All it would take is one moment in which he becomes suddenly visible, therefore intolerable. The wrong sort of look on his face, a grin at the wrong cop, a scowl at the ragpickers' gang leader, next thing he knows, there's another bloody incident in the city. A man like himself? He won't even become a statistic. He is not one of those who are counted.

If the cops came by right now, he risks having his head split open. Nobody will summon a doctor. Nobody will drag him to the government hospital at this time of night. Nobody will write out a death certificate. They will not even call one of those boys who gather the pieces of people cut down by the trains. Nobody will ask why and whom did he ever hurt? He knows, yet he cannot bring himself to hurry. Slowly he moves. Slow as the dawn of a day of leisure.

A Woman Encounters Love in Illicit Places, and Watches Over Her Lover's Wife

This one is a smiling harrumph of a woman and has photos that prove it. She displays her rosy gums, does not press her lips together when a camera is pointed at her. There are hundreds of photos: sitting with Mama, standing with Papa, all of them clustered on the sofa at festivals, with her husband and children and in-laws, and with each of them separately. She has photos with friends from kindergarten, from college, with neighbours from every building she has ever lived in. Everyone has a memory of her rushing into the frame, saying, *Hold on! Me too! Take one with me too!*

Her friends would tilt their heads at pretty fifteen-degree angles to mask their chins. Not she. She tipped her head back and put her large teeth on show. Her husband teases her about her feral smile. *As if you're going to eat the photographer the minute after he takes the photo. What are you so happy about, hmm? So much smiling, for what?*

She blinked when he said it. Her smile was slinking away but she clenched it between her large teeth and up she came again, bubbling with mirth. *You wait and see how I eat you.*

She said it with a laugh. She can say anything to anyone with that smile on her face. Ask anyone. They all say, *Such a lovely person, always smiling.* But really, why does she do it, smile all the time? Ask, and she will blink. Blink-blink. Press her for an answer. She is likely to say that she is busy enjoying life. She might chuck you under the chin. *Smile more, think less. So much thinking, for what?*

This is her motto, she claims. *Don't think too much. Just do whatever you want.* The truth is, she thinks a lot herself. Very hard, very fast. Like the time she took the last train home with her kitty group. She had to think about whether crossing the street to look for a taxi was a better option than taking the skywalk. They were a group of five women and wouldn't fit into one taxi. Two taxis would have to be found. Besides, it was a nice, short walk home. True, there were all kinds of men and stray dogs just outside the railway station but they could take the skywalk. It was quieter, safer, and it took them right down to the bus stop from where it was just half a kilometre to their apartment complex. In less than ten seconds she had made up her mind and taken a left turn on the bridge that led towards the skywalk, before the other ladies could start talking about finding a taxi.

She was walking a step ahead of the others and saw the man moving up-down under the blanket before the rest of the group did. She didn't break her stride. If she had hesitated for the tiniest second, they would all have stopped to look. Having stopped, they would have had to react somehow. Crying out, hissing, making a sound of distress or disgust, even though this is how they have always imagined it—people who sleep on pavements and under bridges, rutting away in the open. This is the picture they conjure and then quickly dismiss when they see waifs begging, newborns strung across their flat chests. Having seen it, they would have felt compelled to enact their shock. But if they cried out, the man might react too. He might roll away, turn around. What next? His thing would be out. They would see it. They would have to pretend not to see. Worse, the man might call out a challenge. *What you looking at? Never done it yourself?*

He might use a bad word. Then they would be forced to retaliate. Not with bad words. That would just render them equals. She knows the group better than to imagine them standing there, slanging with a homeless man with his thing out. No, they would issue vague threats instead, something that affirmed their mutual status. They, respectable middle-class women, and him…he doesn't count. They would have to do something to show him that he dare not challenge women like themselves. On the other hand, if the man took fright, rolled over and revealed the person lying under him, what were they to do?

If it was a younger woman, they could allow themselves a bit of sly derision. *People still commuting and there she is! And not a squeak of protest from her.* If it was an older woman, they would be tempted to say more. A creature of the market who can't afford to say no to homeless men. Reduced to a coin taken from a beggar on the skywalk. One of them might have said it out loud. *Whore!*

And what if it was neither an old woman nor a young one? If it was a child, they would have been forced to do something. Scream. Threaten to call the police. Bring out cell phones, speed-dial husbands, dial the railway police helpline, pour out all the bad words they knew. If the man tried to run away, they would have calmed down a bit, but if he didn't run, it could have gotten worse.

They were all afraid of karma, she knew. They read about incidents in the newspaper. When they called each other, they have all said that such monsters must die. If they did not act after having seen what they saw, they would go home, look at their own children and shiver. They would always remember that they were too squeamish to stop the man on the skywalk, how they let him get away with it. Therefore, with each other as witness, they would have had to kick this man. Stamp on his limbs, his groin. Use their heels.

All these thoughts had flashed across her mind in the few seconds it took her to walk past the man moving up-down, up-down under the blanket. From the corner of an eye, she noticed his matted brown hair and bony ankles. His vigour. She did not exchange a glance or a whisper with the kitty ladies. Eyes fixed on the ribbed metallic floor of the skywalk, she walked fast. The clickety-click of four pairs of heels followed close behind.

She didn't break stride until she had reached the end of the skywalk. Then, one foot poised on the first step of the winding staircase going down, she had turned around to look at her friends. A gurgle in her throat, a sparkle in her eye. A wink. *See how they manage it? Rent-free too! Perched high above us mere mortals! Enjoying themselves on our taxes, isn't it?*

It was a long climb down to street level but the kitty group had laughed and chattered all the way back, the outrage knocked clean out of them. Noses sweating with excitement and the unusual exercise, they complained of falling civic standards, the sufferings of first-class ladies, and cops who don't do their jobs.

Their spirits stayed high until they reached the gate to their apartment complex, when their giggles gave way suddenly.

Security had sauntered up, smiling tentatively. His head tipped forward, peering into their flushed faces. She had smiled back at him even though she knew what the others were thinking. *This fellow is a bit over.* Over-what? None of them has the right word for it. Not over-friendly. Not over-smart. Just something over and above his job. It is embarrassing, this over-ness.

She was alert to the slight chill that was descending on her kitty group as Security smilingly followed them back to the building. She wasted no time in recovering their collective good mood. As they waited for the elevator, she brought out her cell phone. The five of them huddled close and made pouts with lips that had miraculously stayed bright red despite the drinks and dinner. When the elevator arrived, they stepped in with a great susurration of skirts, jangling bangles, clicking heels. They took a few more pictures in the elevator, blowing kisses at their mirrored selves. Later, looking at the photographs, she wondered what the man under the blanket would have made of their dresses, their red painted pouts. How would he caption such a photo?

Annie Zaidi

'Ladies dressed up to attend a bridal shower'. Alternately: 'Ladies of the night'. Flushed faces, wobbly gaits, cleavages on display, the whiff of liquor on their breath. Perhaps he too holds a picture of such women in his mind. Rutting away. Not on the skywalk, of course, but still. In a hotel room or in the beds of men who can afford to hire women over a phone call. How can anyone know what transpires between a woman's legs just by looking at her outdoor self? And how can one stop other people's imaginations? Or their tongues. They'll think what they'll think.

The last thing she does before going to bed is to step into her sixteenth-floor balcony and peer down. It is too dark to spot the tenth-floor balcony, below and to the left of her own. Not that it matters. She knows by heart the rhythms of that apartment. When the first cup of tea is made, how long the television plays, when the bedroom lights are turned off. She already knows that at this hour, only a tiny night light would be spilling out of the bedroom, filtered thick blue through the curtains and not quite reaching the balcony.

She must be the only person in the world interested in the comings and goings of the woman on the tenth floor. That woman, who does not smile back at her, does not castigate her, does not abuse or threaten her with exposure. She merely goes about the business of existing, quietly growing old.

This woman often sits down in front of the dresser and leans towards the mirror, wondering if she herself is growing old at the same rate as the woman on the tenth floor. Afternoons are tricky. She has too much free time on her hands. This is the problem really. Just too much alone time. It sits like a heavy-limbed beast on her hands. On her mouth. On her head. When she lies down, it sits on her chest. When she turns on her side, it crushes her hip bone.

She needs a creative hobby. Not shopping or clubs. Those are not real hobbies. The woman on the tenth floor doesn't have a hobby either. She doesn't even go shopping. Hasn't joined any kitties. Well, good on her. She shouldn't have joined the kitty herself. She looks at the photos from the ladies' night on her phone and allows herself a mad moment. She mentally photoshops the woman from the tenth floor into this gaggle. It doesn't work. An image of that woman in black chiffon and a red pouty mouth refuses to form.

She pictures herself telling that woman, *It's not expensive. Not at all. I got the dress off a stall in Colaba that sells reject export maal from big-big labels. That's how I manage it. Cent per cent French chiffon. You could come with me some time. I'll show you.*

In the photo, the scalloped edge of an electric-blue bra peeks from under the neck of the black chiffon dress she was wearing. She enlarges the photo. Funny that blue should show up under black. Her left breast stands out, a neon shade of midnight blue. She could send the picture to him. He would reply, though not at once. He would see the message tonight but pretend to be asleep, or refuse to look at it until noon. She pictures him cautiously trying out the sound of the words in his mouth, before replying. *That smile!* Or, it might be something worse than that inanity. *God Bless!*

Her own husband, on the other hand, would answer no matter the time. If she sent a sexy picture of herself at midnight, he would call her at dawn, or whenever he happened to wake up. If she answered the phone all groggy, he would have groaned dramatically. *Let me quit this job. Let's just sell the flat and move to a village, eat peanuts for the rest of our lives. Let's run away.* Then she would laugh and call him a dodo. Married people don't run away with each other.

A creak now slithers up the side of the building and she stiffens. She cannot stop stiffening, no matter how many times she hears it. The woman on the tenth floor has stepped out in the balcony. Another sleepless night. That woman will be resting her elbows on the railing, staring at the unblinking city lights until whatever tide has pulled her out at this hour recedes. In ten minutes, or half an hour, the balcony door will creak again and that woman will return to her empty bed. In another minute, she herself will go back in and resume her life. She will not remove her make-up just yet. She likes to let the kids see her as she looked after a night of partying. After waking the children, she will make them a fine breakfast. Something sweet. Then she'll give them their tiffin boxes and wave bye-bye-see-you at the door. She will go back into the balcony and wait until she sees the two kids emerge from the lobby and head towards the gate, where they will wait for their school bus. Once she hears the distinct triple parp of the bus horn, she will shower and go back to bed. She must try to sleep well past noon.

She should start napping more in the afternoons. Time would not hang so heavy on her hands if she could sleep during the day. These afternoons are killer. There's nothing else the matter with her. She must nap. Just thinking the word, nap, felt refreshing. But after she has changed into her nightclothes and settled into bed, she begins to think that she should send a photo of herself to the man from the tenth floor. If she sends it right now, he might reply in the afternoon.

A Security Guard Reflects on Invisible Threats and the Betrayal of Friends

This man sits all night long, knees drawn up, heels resting on the edge of a wooden stool. Age indeterminate, of slight build. He is growing a moustache these days.

Rarely does he carry a stick, though he could if he chose to. Some would prefer that he did; others are not so sure. His job is simply to keep his eyes open. They dare not ask him to do more. If he had a gun, say, he may want to use it. Security people aren't saints. What about that fellow who was involved with a gang and looted his own employer's shop? No, guns are out of the question, they say. Even a stick is not safe. A heavy stick can do a lot of damage. There was that watchman who clubbed a woman to death inside her own flat.

Can they trust that this man would use a stick only when confronted with a robber, a nuisance-maker, an insane displayer of private parts? Can they swear that no nuisance will ever be made by their own children? As for insanity, what household is wholly sane? No, no, violence is not an option a watchman should consider. Not even with a stick. All they need the man for is to keep his eyes open. Keep an account of new faces, in-out timings. Note down vehicle numbers, ask some questions. *Who do you want to meet? What flat number? Purpose of visit? Wait here. No guest parking, nonono guest parking. Read the sign.*

He has been asking for a chair for many days now but they haven't given him one. In a chair, he might sleep even more comfortably. This is a man who nods off on a backless stool. Imagine if he had back support? He'd sleep right through an incident. Still, a consensus cannot be reached. Some of them feel bad that he does not have a chair. They give him other things to make up for it. A plastic bucket with a rusty handle. A new spoon of an in-between size, neither teaspoon nor tablespoon. An olive-green fleece jacket. A synthetic wool blanket with geometric patterns in orange and blue. A plastic keychain in the shape of the Leaning Tower of Pisa. A glass souvenir inscribed with the name of a mid-ranked management college that nobody can find place for in their laden cabinets.

Some of them complain that he is insolent. When they walk past, he looks right at them, straight into their eyes. They don't like his peering, gauging, weighing, level-eyed look. He ought to lower his eyes. A nod would be all right, a salaam, a salute. He need not smile and tilt his head in that familiar way, as a friendly neighbour might. He ought to have been trained about these things.

He does not know, of course, that they say such things. He thinks he is doing a fine job as security. That's what they call him too. Security. He staves off unspecified danger. Non-dangers too, such as unfamiliar cars, and vendors of dry fruit come down from the hills for the winter, bearded men with broken shoes, vendors of electronic gadgets, women with neat partitions in their hair and those wearing cheap plastic slippers, men carrying heavy packages. Often he has stopped them only to discover that they have been summoned by one of the residents. Like the day he stopped those two men at the gate and they turned out to be the police. Now, how can one tell who is what, without a uniform? Those two were in loose white shirts hanging over their trouser belts. They could have been the sort of men who come into a building pretending to be visitors but are actually just staking the place out. He did his job, didn't he?

One of those two turned out to be of inspector rank. Challenged at the gate, he gave Security such a thwack, it almost broke his neck. Afterwards, once they had finished their enquiry, the inspector had paused at the gate and nodded. He had spoken rather nicely. *Good man! You do your job. Pity you're too old to join the force.*

However, he thinks, he has not done a good job. That sixteenth-floor incident, he didn't see it coming. Such a good woman too. She used to call out 'Security! Security!' for the smallest bit of trouble. When the lift was not working, when she needed the water valve turned on for a few extra minutes, when the garbage man failed to show up, she would call out. Why did she not call out that day? Not even one scream.

Nowadays, he thinks a lot about danger. Look at those French windows. Balcony so high, railings so low. This urban habit of hovering so far above the earth. It is not healthy. Unnatural. The earth was given to us as sanctuary. God intended for us to have our feet touch earth at all times. So far from Mother Earth, how can anyone feel safe?

He doesn't understand the charm of this up-up-up lifestyle. Every day, he wakes up at noon and the first thought in his head is that he can't wait to get off the terrace. They allow him to sleep up there in a tiny shed with a toilet attached and it is a better deal than he's had in the city up until now. Still, he doesn't feel right until he has come downstairs and can feel his feet on the ground again. Reflecting upon housing and architecture is not his job though. His job is to keep his eyes open, to look out for danger. In this, he has failed. Not just this once. He's failed before. On the last job, he had failed so badly, he didn't wait for the management to fire him. He quit as soon as the rains arrived and the construction work came to a halt.

What slippery mud a man is made of! His own friend. How many cups of tea had they had together? Squatting on the ground, lighting a little fire, smoking a bidi. How many times had they cooked a simple meal together on his kerosene stove? Dozens of times. A hundred times. Two months of standing about in that empty lot with nothing but a 'No Trespassing' sign and a metal fence for company. Then these people show up, speaking a dialect he recognizes. Listening to his friend was like watching slow curls of smoke rise up from a distant hill. The pair of them. His friend and his wife. Didn't they laugh softly as they waited for his wife to finish cooking their one-pot meal? How many times did he hold their baby in his lap? Didn't he sigh with gratitude afterwards?

Walking about the construction site alone while they slept, he had persuaded himself that he wasn't just guarding an empty lot, a load of bricks and iron, bamboo and rope. He was guarding the workers too. He had paced, careful not to make a sound, for he knew the sun always rose a little too soon. The night never quite finished mending their broken muscles. He had even started to buy three cups of morning tea, so they might be spared the trouble of going to fetch milk at dawn.

To turn on him like that, and for what? A length of metal. It would fetch, what? Maybe just enough to feed a family for a few weeks. Was he to sell himself so cheap? So that another man's family could eat a few meals they didn't work for?

Oh, never mind the meals. He doesn't want to think about the meals they shared, cooked by a woman he used to call Bhabhi. This city is always being built and broken down and rebuilt. Was he to look the other way from their petty thieving just because they were friendly? They didn't know him if that's who they thought he was. And the gall of that man! That brother-in-law of his, the curly-headed fellow with a sweet smile? Calling him 'brother' when he first caught them red-handed, then kicking him in the shin before running off.

Judging from the outside, nobody can tell which

man or which woman carries a secret cargo of violence. He knows this now. Still, he tries to look for signs. Peering into faces, levelling his eyes with theirs, reading their pursed lips, he tries to get his measure of the danger within.

An Adulterous Man Revisits the Truth After His Lover Falls to Her Death

This man is walking circles around the building he had moved out of, swearing never to return. Yet here he is, the second time this month.

Nobody will ask questions, of course. They will not even notice. Most people don't know their neighbours in the city. People are always coming and going, tenants like himself. Eleven months and the lease expires. A new family moves in, a polite nod is exchanged in the lobby or elevator. Politely, they are forgotten. He lived here eight years though, and his old neighbours recognized him the last time. They'd come up to talk and he had begun to talk up his new place like a fool.

Even to his own ears, he was sounding like a real estate agent. *Seven hundred and fifty square foot carpet area. All amenities within two hundred metres. Whatever the builder promised. Park view, swimming pool, gym, full facilities. Good investment. Great investment!* The words had dropped from his lips like pigeon shit on lamp posts. He knew they were listening with half an ear, impatient to sidle away. Thankfully, they did not ask what brings him back here. People in this city know how to mind their own business. They must have assumed he was visiting his ex-wife and that was perfect because he knew that she never talks to any of the neighbours. Of course, you never know with women. Totally unpredictable. Who could have imagined that she would want to stay on here once he had left?

The way she used to go on and on about leaving this pigeonhole flat. Now here she is, a year later. Same flat. The furniture is the same too. Not that he ever visits. The sixteenth-floor woman had kept him updated. He never did understand. He didn't like to talk about his wife, not at all. He had said so. *I don't care. I don't care. Nothing to do with me.* Yet, she kept calling him to supply endless detail. The colour of his wife's new clothes, the model of car she has bought, the time she returns from work. He should have told her to stop calling. He should never have taken her calls.

His wife has turned out to be stranger than he had imagined possible. True, the landlord was abroad and kept the rent low since he couldn't be bothered to find new tenants. Still, would any normal woman stay in the same place after her husband had walked out on her? A rented flat, for god's sake! She had always hated it. Why didn't she just go back to her parents' house? His mother had warned him to keep a sharp eye on the bitch. His lawyer warned him too. Wives are sure to dig in their claws. Not his wife though.

How strange she had turned out to be. *When you want a divorce, just ask.*

No talk of money or alimony. Now she has got herself a job, bought herself a new car. Now she watches TV alone. Same old television set. The sixteenth-floor woman had told him, with a laugh, *Your wife makes me nervous and envious at the same time.*

That was another crazy one. Turned out to be crazy after all. With her gummy smile and her practical view of marriage, she had been his idea of what a normal wife was like. Normal clothes. Normal make-up. Normal home decor. Ugly ceramic flowers, glittering deities painted on squares of cardboard, inspirational quotes printed and hung in plastic frames in every room. He had gone up to the sixteenth floor so often, he knew each niche, each cushion cover. He always noticed when she bought something new to add to the clutter. He had even asked once, *Who pays for all this junk?*

The reply came a little too quick. *Not you. Is that not enough?*

Had a tongue on her. Worse than his wife perhaps. He ought to have been warned by that. She was not the weepy, whiny kind though. Her voice was light, soft as soap bubbles. His grey moods would disappear at the lightest touch of her fingers. She had a good life, she said so herself. Her husband wouldn't divorce her, not even if he found out. The flat had been bought in her name. There were the two children. She was content, didn't she say so herself?

He had a call from her just the day before she did it. She said nothing to warn him. Her voice was a bit subdued but he thought he knew what that was about. He had told her that they should take some time off. *Think about how things stand, how it'll look. I mean, I don't live downstairs now so it's not like I can come and go easily, just a few seconds in the elevator, and nobody noticing. Your children are growing up. Just think about it for a while.*

How long since their last call? Maybe two weeks? Or was it closer to a month? That subdued 'hello', then a whole minute of silence. He did tell her that she could come over to his place if she wanted to. Now his mother was no more, it was possible. How glad he is now that she didn't come over after all. These days they hound a man for nothing. CCTV, security, phone call records. He could have been in jail. It was sheer luck that she did not come over, and that he too had stopped visiting her months ago. The courts were not likely to understand that it had nothing to do with him. Can a man expect justice in this system?

It was a narrow miss. Very narrow.

Yet he has come back to this building. Her building. Twice in the same month. For what? He has rehearsed answers in case anyone asks. He needs a document signed by his wife. Ex-wife. Soon to be formal and legal and a done deed. Then he will change the subject and begin to talk about his new flat. *Property prices will double in two years. The timing was right for me. Luck, you know. Certain things just work out. And certain things do not work out despite every effort.* Then he will tell the listener what his late mother used to say. *Your wife will be the death of me.*

Mother's words will roll off his tongue. The bitch hadn't earned a single rupee in eight years. She'd have swallowed him whole and burped up a curse if he hadn't left when he did. *It was impossible. Couldn't eat a meal in peace. My old mother couldn't watch TV in peace. Is that a life? It was my mother who chose her, of course. Mother did all the looking, selecting, approving, negotiating before my marriage. Poor lady, god bless her. Such a blunder!*

It is the sort of thing he can say to other men. They will shake their heads, or stare down at their shoes. It may not be a bad idea to bump into a neighbour after all. He can ask how things are. He will not ask directly. That would be disastrous. He can just appear to be curious. It is natural to gossip a little. *There was some incident, no? I saw the name of the building in the newspaper.*

He would not mention the sixteenth floor of course. The slightest rumour could bring trouble to his door. The police can make your life hell even without a formal complaint. People are always looking for opportunities to harass decent folk. He has a job with a multinational firm now. He is paying monthly instalments on the new flat. His wife is not dragging him through the family court, not yet. She is a mad woman though. Who knows what will happen when he asks her to sign the divorce papers? He shouldn't push his luck right now.

That's what she used to say too. Standing in that sixteenth-floor balcony, with her hands on the railing and hips swaying side to side as if there was a piece of music playing inside her body, she would say, *Don't push it. You don't know your luck. Your wife is a gem.*

He had snorted. *If there was a child, the bitch would have had me by the throat. A child is a leash in the hands of a wife. She can make you her dog, her donkey, her performing monkey.*

It was true, wasn't it? Thinking of the husband

from the sixteenth floor sends a little shiver through this man's frame. All the poor fellow did was make good money so his wife could spend it. What would her husband be doing now? Did he look the same, the way he looked in the photos? Dozens of photographs all over the house—him and her, his mother and her mother, and all of them with the children. Where are the children now?

In a way, he reflects, he has been lucky. If he had had children, he could not have left so easily. His wife had made a huge scene about it once. She had called his mother an old witch who had put a curse on her womb. That night, she had wept a long time. *I can't bear it*, she had sobbed. *Can't bear it any longer. Take me away from this house, I can't bear it.*

Well, she didn't need to bear it. He had sent her packing. Or rather, he packed himself off along with his mother. Luckily, his wife did not make a scene or threaten to file a domestic violence case. Lucky too that he had never laid a hand on her. These days, the laws are all geared towards women. They only have to point a finger and the husband is finished. Locked out of his own house and paying through his nose to maintain a woman who doesn't want him in the first place.

That one's husband, for example. He must be petrified. Bad enough that such a thing should happen. There must have been a lot of questions. Police. Lawyers. He himself was shitting bricks because she had called him the day before it happened. For her husband, it was a very close call. They could accuse him of anything. But finally, the papers reported it as a freak accident. She was watering her potted plants. The tiles in the balcony were slippery. The railing was not high enough.

Who can say what happened? It could even be that. She must have wanted to see him though, why else would she call? She was content, she used to say, but perhaps not so content after all. Why was she seeing him? What was wrong with her? With the children right there.

This man now strolls past the building where he spent eight years and stops to nod at the watchman. It is a new fellow. He doesn't recognize the man as a former resident and turns up the palm of his hand, fingers curved into a question. *Where do you think you're going?*

He hesitates, nearly turns away, then turns and begins to read the names on the wall of the lobby. Flat number, name, flat number, name. He jabs the air with his finger, then turns to face the watchman. *Isn't this B Wing?*

He keeps his face carefully impassive as a sliver of suspicion enters and falls out of the watchman's eyes. *This is C Wing, sir. Turn right and five steps, and there it is. Who do you want to meet?*

Just as well, this man thinks, he hasn't run into anyone familiar. No need to bring up the incident. It was just as the report said, a freak accident. What does it have to do with him?

A Trinket Seller Accepts Treats from a Snake Charmer While her Husband Languishes in Jail

This woman no longer lives on a pink cloud. Instead, she has learnt to say, *Move on, you! Go on, move ahead! And mind your head.*

She is the only woman of her tribe who switched to a salwar suit instead of a sari once the skirts they had on when they left the village were worn ragged at the waist and hem. Her cousins wept over their torn skirts, and the impossibility of finding a tailor to make skirts like these. Or about finding the money for tailors. They even said that they wanted to go back to the village. As if it was merely a question of turning around, finding a state transport bus, and walking the remaining distance back to their thatched huts. As if the thorn trees, the huts that were never locked, the waterwheel, the nearly dry well would still be standing there, waiting. As if they only had to toss their ragged bundles into a corner, pick up a staff, and go looking for a camel to milk. She sometimes thinks she is the only one who managed to get off her cloud with her head intact.

Most people lose their heads when they're pushed off their cloud. Her sister-in-law had once grabbed another woman at the paid public toilet. Grabbed her by the hair and shaken her like a rag doll. There were clumps of hair in her fists by the time she let go. If she hadn't dragged her sister-in-law away from the toilet before the other woman could gather her relatives, there would have been a riot.

Her sister-in-law is fierce, like a hawk. She used to envy those piercing amber eyes, the strength of her arms, and the speed at which she could swoop down on those who crossed her. She herself was a hothead once, but she has learnt since that, in this city, it is better to use your mouth rather than your fists. *Go, go on, hey! Yeah, you show me whatever you want to show me, and then I'll show you something too. Go home while you can.*

That's what they've taught her. In this city, you don't hold your tongue. You have to start talking much, much before your blood begins to rise. Don't let it get into your eyes. Spit it out. Words are the long rope people give each other in this city. Cursing takes the edge off their rage. Warning others not to get above themselves allows them to look past the daily humiliations they are subject to.

Where she grew up, words were song. Words were their special hoard, the one thing they could not lose. In her heart, they remain plump and vivid—sheep, wool, berries, snakes. Two dozen words for cloud. Soft, playful words for camel. What is the word for this feeling of craning her neck backwards, squinting at a cloud, and seeing in it the shape of her destiny? These are not things to which anyone gives tongue. Not among her people. Her people would keep their tongues rolled up tight inside their mouths. A man who speaks all day is as bad as one who sleeps all day.

In this city, there are long strings of words in every mouth. Clank-clank like the wheels of the train. The short thread of abuse and the long jasmine garland of seduction when they are trying to sell you things. *Costs nothing to look. Come here, who else will make you a heroine for a hundred? Honey's waiting. Where's the money? Fifty-fifty, I'm calling it quits! Take it away for fifty, I want to go home too. It's late, come on, do us both a favour. It's prettier than your fantasies, come take it. Come loot me, my love. Better than kidneys, that's what this stuff is, I tell you. Better than kidneys and liver, both.*

It used to make her dizzy, the noisy wit of boys selling things on the street. Their eyes shredded fine with laughter. Only two of the middle buttons done up on their shirts, colourful vests within. She didn't always understand the words they hurled at passers-by but she understood how it worked. They made people feel alive—their cries, their senseless exaggerated metaphors, their grins, the way they tossed their wares up in the air and caught them carelessly, as if to say, *See? It's just a thing. What's a little money? Nothing.*

She knows she will never be able to do this. The only thing she has learnt from such boys is abuse delivered deadpan and the art of sidestepping a fight. *Go, go, get on your way.* She has not yet learnt clever twists of language. Nobody smiles at her. A few men do, but those are not smiles that sustain the heart. She can drive a hard bargain though. Her hard desert eyes know the art of looking at a woman and reading the strength of desire in a pair of wary eyes. No matter how hard they try to beat her down, she always knows who among them has her heart set on a blue bead necklace and who will allow herself to buy the white metal hairpin that costs twice as much as the ordinary black one. Her daughter may grow up lacking even this ability. Already the mite looks about herself with restless, empty eyes, as if she isn't sure what she's doing here. Those eyes never stop on a face for more than a second. Not yet talking though she is nearly two years old. The snake charmer is right. She may as well loan the girl out. Let the child earn her keep.

If he takes the child along, she will not have to watch her all day. She need not be tied to this one spot in the market. She sold many more neck-pieces when she wandered street to street. Now she has to carry the baby in a sling. Getting heavier by the month. Starting to toddle off on her own too. She cannot look away for a moment with all these cars and all these people. If the girl's father were here, she could have gone to work in peace. He knew how to hold a child, even in his sleep.

This is another curse. Remembering the moment. The frisson in her limbs when she felt his eyes on her back. Turning around, meeting his gaze, seeing the baby tucked into his side. Knowing that instant, knowing right down to her ankle bones that she would linger. She would wait there until he said a word to her. Maybe he would give her something—a drink of water, the baby to hold, a sweet to suck on.

The memory of their first encounter stands tall, shiny, towering above everything else that happened after. Like the new building over there with its hundreds of lit windows stacked up high, high, high. At night, the windows twinkle as if they were neighbours to the stars. Far below, there is grime and old moss on the walls of blackened old mills, and shops where not a single customer walks in all day. Further below, other memories lie pooled. Leaving the construction site below which her own tribe had huddled under scaffolding and plastic sheets. Watching the rain pour and pelt, shivering in their fading odhnis and ragged, close-pleated skirts. The men with their turbans wound tight, moustaches proudly upturned. Still proud, still talking of returning to tend the sheep before winter. She left all of that, exchanging it for a spot under a strange little rail that runs high above the ground. As if there was any sense to it. But she had been floating on her own cloud then. Pink cloud of dream, her mother said. *That's all it is. You're sitting on a pink cloud. It will rain itself empty when the next monsoon comes around.*

Better than a grey cloud that never rains. It was the first retort she had delivered to her mother. First and last. None of her tribe said anything further. Their silence was absolute and she read it correctly to mean that she could no longer count on them.

It had not mattered. Her man was enough. Her heart filled to see that her man was skilled, and resourceful. It took six months to gather the right sort of plastic, rags, and broken bits of wood but it took him just one day to turn it into a home. That is another gleaming memory. A shining beam of a day that warms her even now: the sight of him arching, weaving, knotting, measuring the space that would be their home against the span of his lean arms. How he worked! A hut in one day. Who among her tribe had ever done that?

He had also made another little shelter using old flex fabric and bamboo at the construction site where his sister worked. Then one night, his sister's husband came and took him away. There was an opportunity, he said, at the site. A lot of new material had arrived and it was lying in a heap, out in the open air. His brother-in-law had said there would be no trouble; he was friends with the security guard. All they had to do was pick up some lengths of twisted metal ropes to sell as scrap. Two hours of work. It'll see us through the season, he had said. She hadn't had the sense to ask at the time—see us through how many seasons if they failed?

Winter came. Then summer. Then the rains. She had waited through the long nothing that followed. A flat, stinking nothing. A rope of metal twisted around her heart. Yet, she had clung to her pink cloud. She teetered on the edge of it, clinging to the wisp of a shelter, her belly swelling. If it was not for the fact that his sister was as bewildered as herself and weeping into her infant son's chest all night, she would have thought herself abandoned and a fool for waiting. They had no phones. There was no word about what had happened until her sister-in-law found the courage to go back to the construction site and ask a few questions. Yes, the guard had raised the alarm. Yes, both the men were taken. Yes, there was a police case.

She began to wait for the police to let him go. How many ropes of metal could he have carried? Why did the police not offer him the chance to perform a penance and a fine? He could work for them until he had paid back the value of what he took. That's how people settled matters in her tribe. If they let him work, he could have paid back ten times the price of that damn metal by now. Nobody gained anything by keeping a man like him in jail. She was certain that they would see the sense of it in a few weeks and set him free.

She got off her cloud only after the city came at her with a bulldozer. She would have laughed at them, needing a great beast of a machine to rip down a sheet of plastic and a few twigs. Her man would have done it in two minutes with his bare hands. It was a sparrow's nest of a home. They only had to ask and she could have stamped it down with her own feet. The bulldozer was a cruel joke but she couldn't afford to smile. She was suddenly on the footpath with a big belly and the rains due to start in a month.

His sister went back to work on a construction site, leaving her with the infant to watch and instructions to go begging on the street whenever the traffic signal turned red. She was to carry her nephew on her hip and say, he's hungry, then to point to her own big belly and say, please. It was true enough; the child was hungry. She was too.

Something for the child. I've got to feed him. I've had nothing to eat all day. Let him eat a bite. Sister. Brother. Mother, five rupees. She said the words, but could not bring herself to put her hand out. She would stand outside car windows, the child on her hip and her eyes burning red. In the evenings, she would sit under a tree with her burden of bead necklaces and there she remained, right up to the hour of birthing.

Her sister-in-law's boy is growing fast and is quick of tongue. Quick on his legs too. She doesn't have to carry him any more. He knows how to dart between cars when the light turns red, and has learnt not to go in front of buses. The driver cannot see him and the passengers are too high for him to be able to touch their elbows. He brings in enough coins for his keep. She cannot do much more work herself, between watching her own baby, working beads into necklaces, painting clay lamps and glittering tin vases with pictures of the gods on them. It doesn't add up to three meals though. People in this city don't stop bargaining, driving down her price even if it is images of their own gods they're looking at.

Well, the gods aren't going to mind her daughter nor feed her. She may as well go with the snake charmer's offer. He is not a bad man, just that he never learnt to do anything except catch snakes. There are such men in the world. They learn one trade well and they practise it with a passion that ruins them for all other work. Her own man, after all, never went to work on the construction site. He'd rather lie in the mud and mind a baby, letting his sister carry bricks instead. It wasn't like he minded the heavier work. If he could weave and build a shelter for us, he could also work on the knots for scaffolding and get paid for it. If he could carry off those blighted metal rods in the middle of the night, he could just as easily have worked for the same contractor, carrying rods and bags of cement on the site. They could have eaten better. But no, he would rather go pick up bits and pieces of people cut down on the railway tracks.

That's steady work too, he used to say. *At least one*

body every other day on this line. It paid poorly though. Much less than construction work. Ghastly work. And besides, he was a fool about those bodies. He never brought back a gold ring or a purse that had fallen on the tracks. Then why did he go and steal cheap iron rods to sell off in the scrap market? The biggest fool in this city, she bets. Two years now, and he's never held his own daughter in his arms, not even once. This damned snake charmer has to come around and carry her about.

She lets him. There's no harm in it. He's sure to give the girl a lick of opium to keep her quiet. Sometimes she thinks she wouldn't mind a lick herself. Or a puff from the snake charmer's chillum. His black eyes and black shirt and that sweet smoke hanging in the air when he comes around. He tosses her nephew up in the air, and the boy laughs. He is almost her own son now, for it is she who bathes him and feeds him, and takes the coins from his little hands. It is her heart that beats hard when the traffic light changes, she who worries when he doesn't move fast enough.

The snake charmer is smart. He knows how to turn her no to a yes. He never makes for her own baby all at once. First, he plays with her nephew, showing him colourful balloons. Twisting them into the shape of a monkey or a dog. Then, when the boy has begun to chortle and run circles around him, only then does he pick up the girl. He remembers, always, to bring a sweet of some sort. Not just for the children. For her too. Once or twice, he has even brought her a fistful of raw rice tied up in the end of his gamcha. And asking nothing in exchange. He takes nothing from her. Until, one day, when she catches herself thinking, here is a man and not such a bad man either.

Annie Zaidi

A Man with a Dead Wife Comes Upon a Balloon Seller and a Baby

Your car is in the garage and you have had to take an auto rickshaw back home today. You stop at the paanwallah's kiosk to pick up the four cigarettes you allow yourself every day, and that's when you see him, pushing a pram, a bunch of red balloons bobbing above his left shoulder. In the pram is a sleeping child, about two years old. Probably a girl, though you can't tell for sure. A toddler in a frock of indeterminate colour, a tangle of locks over earlobes pierced with a silver wire, the ends of which have been twisted into a knot.

He walks a few steps ahead of you and, once he reaches the gate leading to your building, he stops and turns. You see now that he is a small, dark man. Eyes lined with the blackest kohl, head wrapped in an unfussy turban. Not quite a turban actually. That word suggests yards of crisp fabric, colourful, tie-dyed perhaps. What he wears is a woollen gamcha wrapped around stringy hair. Now a filthy brown-black, that cloth had never set out to be any kind of joyful colour. His eyes are the same shade of brown and you cannot help thinking, these are eyes a woman would fall hard for. You don't know why you think this. Whose filthy brown eyes have you ever paid attention to?

You wonder about the child. You've heard stories.

Annie Zaidi

Kidnapped kids. Drugged kids. Beggar mafia. It's an elaborate set-up. Still, the child does not appear to be starved. No protruding, malnourished belly. The hour is late, past nine. Kids don't fall asleep so easily these days. They watch television until midnight. But this kid is a baby. Out all day in this heat, she should have been howling by now. He must have sedated her. A lick of good old opium perhaps. To his credit, the man is not making her walk. He is, however, asking you for money.

He offers a balloon first. But who wants a balloon at this hour? It is understood that he will ask for money now. He will say the child has not had a morsel all day. He knows you expect him to ask for money. You know that he knows, but you also know that children must be fed, whether or not people buy balloons. It is possible that he tried to sell balloons all day long, and failed. The world is changing so fast. Children are no longer pleased with balloons or seashells. Five-year-olds want smartphones. Games that require no playmates.

Balloons are fragile things, dying on a poor man's shoulder as easily as a flower wilts. Still, you hesitate. Why does he carry around such a small child if not to gain sympathy? But maybe he has no place to leave the child. You remember your own desperation, not knowing what to do with the kids once their mother was gone. There was nobody to pick them up after school. There was nobody to open the door for them when they returned from school. Nobody to feed them lunch or ask them to finish their homework. You had to quit your job for a whole year. You hadn't saved up that much money. Not to account for a whole year of being out of work.

Maybe this man's woman left him, quite literally, holding the baby. He looks like he might be one of those men who marry for love. Check out all that kohl. You've never seen a man wear so much kohl. What sort of man is he? A man who can pick up a noisy, shitting bundle of need, hold it clasped to his chest for hours? Possible. A man who blows up balloons for other people's kids.

On the other hand, it could be a borrowed child. He could be forcing some other poor kid to blow up the balloons. You can't just look at a man's face and decide. These are complicated balloons. A small child wouldn't be able to do it on his own. Twisted into the shape of a monkey and a bicycle, and a big one—a monkey riding a bicycle. He used to buy such balloons when they took the kids to the beach on Sundays.

Annie Zaidi

The man is asking you for flour now. He does not want a coin, he says. He wants to go home and cook. He needs flour, lentils, and vegetables. He hesitates before the word 'vegetable' and, in a flash, you guess that he has meat on his mind. But nobody dares beg for meat, not even in the name of a hungry child. You turn to look at the building beyond the gate. All sixteen floors are warm boxes of yellow light. Nobody's home but your window is a warm yellow slit, like everyone else's. You always leave one light on, so your welcome home is not too bleak.

Suddenly, you want to be done with this man and his dying balloons. Security is alert, having spotted you standing, talking to a man who looks like he could be a nuisance. He saunters up to the gate, watching your eyes for a signal. Should he shoo away the fellow?

The balloon man again asks. *Wheat flour.* His eyes are smokier under the street lamp. They make you think of opium dens although you have never actually been inside one. You imagine it to be a round room rather than a square one, crisscrossed with wreaths of smoke, a huddle of chor-charsi-afeemchis. When you were little, your mother used to warn you against chor-charsi-afeemchis, men who lure children away with sweets. Or balloons.

You try to mentally calculate how much flour is needed to fill two stomachs, but you haven't rolled enough dough this past year to know the answer to that. A kilo of flour costs more money than you are willing to part with. Besides, you don't want to take the trouble of walking to the grocer's shop to buy a bag of flour. A balloon would cost less, but you have already said that you don't want a balloon. You could just give him some loose change, but he has already said he doesn't want money. He wants to go home and cook for the child.

When and how did this man learn to cook? Who taught him? You are still struggling with the kneading of the dough. Your chapattis are neither round nor soft. You burn the food a lot. You wonder if the man even has a stove to cook on. Probably not. Yet, he must be cooking for himself at least. Or does he, too, get by on greasy restaurant food and the sympathy of friends? You search his face for clues, for evidence that he knows what you now know. A lot of people loving you a little does not fill the shrinking pool of calm in your chest. Little dribbles of how-are-yous, feet shuffling around you, artfully tipping their always-here-for-yous. Shoulders, arms, heart emoticons on text. These are not a grip on life. Shrieking long dinners with parents. They're a port of call, not a harbour. They want you to give up your sixteenth-floor apartment, as if it were infectious.

They're not wrong. Grief is a pox. Between apartments, between friends, you have learnt to read fear in their gestures. Concern, of course, and pity, but also fear. Like the time when your college gang found out that a classmate had tested positive for HIV. You all tried so hard to be cheerful, invited her to all your parties, but they couldn't help looking at her just a second too long. At the plates she ate off, the rugs she sat on. You too. It wasn't infectious, you knew, but you couldn't see beyond what had happened to her. Couples held hands tighter in her presence. As they do around you now, after what's happened.

The balloon man is still looking at you, smoky eyes glistening with hope. A sort of dread too. What dreadful thing does he see in your face? You notice now that he is a slight man. Much smaller than you. He must be all ribs under that black shirt. What sort of man is he, under his clothes? Perhaps he is the sort of man to whom a woman is attracted for reasons nobody else can fathom. Sickly thin. Filthy hands. Greasy hair. Bad breath. Blackened toenails.

You suddenly don't want to give him a bag of

flour. You want to toss him a coin and if he doesn't want it, he can go to hell. You don't move though. *Where is your woman?*

The man slowly blinks his kohl-darkened eyes. *My woman?*

He is weighing you up with his filthy brown eyes. You know he is going to say that she is dead. That is exactly what he says. *Dead. Gone.* Liar! But there is no reason to accuse him of lying. Women die. Some die young. In accidents. In childbirth. Some die out of sheer bloody-mindedness. Like that stupid woman, the wife of one of your colleagues. Crossing the railway tracks with the kids. You felt so bad for him, you actually went for the prayer meet even though you were not a close friend. You barely knew this colleague. He was only a shop manager, not even a regional head. Still, you went to his place along with some of the other guys from the office.

There were blown up photographs sitting on dining chairs that had been turned out and set against the wall. A photo of the woman from her wedding day, her face powdered to make her look three shades lighter. She must have made for a ghostly bride. The kids' photos were recent. There was one where they're splashing about in water, probably at a water park.

Their grandfather had been distraught, howling out loud. *Both of them! She had to take both! Why did she have to take both?*

You remember coming home early for once, telling your wife about it. You must have sounded vehement. *What do you gain by crossing railway tracks instead of taking the bridge? You save, what, a minute? Two minutes? Brainless creature!* Your wife had given you a look that made you press on. *Just imagine, an educated woman. Not some poor, illiterate thing from a village. She'd been to college. And those kids! Can you imagine? This guy, suddenly he's left with nothing. Not even his kids.*

Your wife had smiled when you said this. An odd, bitten-down smile, different from her usual wide-open, gummy smile. Now you remember, you had wondered but had not asked her what that smile was about. Now you're thinking, you should have asked. You should have insisted on knowing.

A Manager
Picks Up
Scraps
of Other
People's
Lives, and
Attempts to
Restore Her
Own

This woman sits on the sofa and watches television, three straight hours, six nights a week. On the seventh day, she watches television all day long and when it is nearing dinner time, she goes to visit her parents.

There used to be two television sets in this flat. There used to be three people living in this flat. None of them could bear the other's taste. That word, taste. *Your taste is vulgar. Your taste is old. Your taste is slow.* As if tastes had life spans and arthritic knees. She watches without comment or complaint, flipping channels to look for something better, or newer, but ultimately, whatever's playing is fine. Advertisements for shampoo and skimmed milk, politicians, movies, the endless soaps.

True, nothing much happens in these soaps. Give up watching for a week and when you come back to it, you find that the story has not moved. That used to be one of his pet complaints. *But nothing really happens in your godawful shows. The way they drag on and on!*

She did not have the right counter-argument at the time. Now she does. Nothing much happens in real life either, does it? But when something does happen, it's a big deal. A wedding. An accident. A divorce. A baby. If any one of these things happened to you, it wouldn't end neatly. It would drag on for years. The soaps are quite realistic, she could argue. But there is nobody to hear her arguments. Not that she remembers too many arguments. Towards the end, when she suggested a change of channel, he would simply say, *I bought you a second TV, didn't I? Watch whatever you like.*

Technically, this was not true. He had not bought her a second TV. He had only bought the second set, not the first one. His mother used to complain that his wife was not letting her watch her beloved programmes in peace. That's the word the old woman had used: programmes.

She is sorry about the whole business now. Those foolish remote-control battles. She was not herself at the time. It was so unlike her to point to household objects and say, *This is mine.* But at the time, she had felt driven to say it. *The TV is mine. It came with my dowry.*

Her dowry! Such a fraught enterprise. How much her parents had worried about giving just enough so that she was seen as a catch, but not so much that the in-laws tasted blood. Crockery set. Clothes. TV. But no car. You can't stop giving once you have given the groom a car. It would be a house next. You heard of such cases all the time. Nobody talked about it, of course, not until it had turned into a police case. If she survived, the 'bride' lay charred in some public hospital, then spent the rest of her youth in surgeries and milling about the courts.

Well, that did not happen to her. Come to think of it, nothing much happened to her. Wedding. Husband. Bedroom. Kitchen. The old woman and her programmes. A lot of boredom. There were pregnancies. Miscarriages. The first one at three months, the second one at two months. She had barely registered the changes that were happening to her body before it was all over. As the old woman kept saying, *But nothing actually happened.*

She is just not a happening girl, she reflects. That was a word they were using a lot when she was in school. A city was happening, or it was not. A restaurant was happening, or it was not. A guy was a happening guy, or not. When she first moved here, young people were still talking of it as a happening city. Her husband spoke of it with pride. *It's hot and happening. You'll see.* Later, he was less proud. By then, he had learnt the stealthy ways in which time fails men like him. A job that only afforded you enough time and money so you could keep doing that job. Stay alive so you can stay alive. Slavery, really. You just waited for better things. Waited to find a new job if you lost the old one. Waited to come home from a job after you'd found it. Waited for an excuse to disrupt the boredom of everything.

Boredom. That's what it was about. She sees it now. Her husband too had been bored. Their mutual complaints had got boring. Meanwhile, time sped up all around them. Sixty seconds of each minute were crammed with sixty-one incidents in the life of the city. Sometimes she thought that if just one more thing were to happen, time itself would lay down in the middle of a busy road and wait to be run over. It would not be run over, of course, because the traffic would not move. The lights would not change. By the time you changed gears, hit the accelerator, the poor thing would have dusted itself off, wandered back into the red electronic timer on top of the next traffic signal. 39, 38, 37....

She counts down every day, impatient like everyone else. Now she doesn't have to kill time. Time doesn't hang heavy on her hands. She considered giving up the car to save time. The car makes her feel like a sparrow in a metal cage with the city as her feed bowl. Besides, she has heard colleagues talking about travelling in trains. Intimate, non-intrusive clusters of friendship that form and unform easily, especially in the ladies' compartment. She might like that. On the other hand, the physical evidence of a thousand bodies was too much for her. Flowers on braids, silver rings on toes, gaudy hair clips, sweat-soaked t-shirts, fake leather bags, scarred abdomens, pimpled backs. Too much, too close.

Colleagues envy her the car. They asked if she was paying off instalments and she confessed, no. It was bought outright. They were surprised, but had not said anything further. Not even, *Wow! How lucky!* They assume her husband has a fancy job and is indulgent. They know she couldn't have bought it outright on her salary.

True enough. She couldn't have bought it outright. Her parents have paid for the car. They have also bought her a new bed. *One daughter has cost you two dowries*, she jokes. Her parents do not like her joking in this way. They would have given her a second dowry if it could have saved her marriage. They blame themselves. They have failed in their parenting. A well-brought-up girl doesn't tell her husband that she can't bear to go on in this way, nor does she remind her mother-in-law about what she brought with her as dowry. Besides, the failure of her womb was no small thing. She should have thought of how much her husband was suffering.

Sometimes she lashes back. *Indeed, you have failed at parenting. The least you could have done for me is to find a husband who could afford to buy his own TV and fridge.*

The fridge too had been a gift, although it didn't come with the dowry. Her parents gave it to her two years after the wedding. After the first miscarriage. Her mother-in-law had made a comment about how some women just sit at home and eat, breaking bread until the oven goes bust, but they can never be counted on to add anything to the household. She had gone back to her parents' house, weeping. So they bought her a fridge. Something was added to the household.

In her lighter moments, she considers writing a letter of appreciation to the manufacturer. The fridge has outlasted her marriage. Come to think of it, most of her dowry items have lasted. The TV set, this sofa on which she continues to sit. When he left, her husband took his mother, the second TV, and all the bedroom furniture, which was all he had brought into their home. The old woman would not take any of the kitchen things. *Let her keep it. These girls bring one ugly set of plates in their dowry and they are ready to send you to jail for eating off them.*

The old woman didn't last four months in that new flat her son bought. Dead. She is not sad about her mother-in-law's death. She is not happy either. It is hard to unspool the magnetic tape of memory. Warm afternoons, trials of old recipes, gossip about three generations of family on either side, graphic accounts of miscarriages in every branch of the family, fifty-year-old cosmetic jewellery handed down, television remote-control battles. She has no word for this kind of remembrance. The old woman is a hard gob stuck in her throat.

The sixteenth-floor woman had watched her face intently when she brought down the news. Perhaps she was looking for signs of ugly pleasure, or a pretend grief. Her husband had not called to inform her. She had to hear about her own mother-in-law's death from an outsider. From the sixteenth-floor woman. Any normal woman would have been driven mad, but not her. After a moment, she had found her tongue. *Thank you for letting me know.*

She had shut the door with a polite click but that woman had some nerve. She came down again that night, this time with a dinner plate. Mindful of tradition, she was playing the good neighbour, bringing food since the bereaved family does not cook on the day someone dies. It was odd. She had not cooked, after all, even though the old woman was no longer family and the death had occurred elsewhere.

She too had been determined to hold up her end of the charade. She had accepted the dish gracefully. She let that woman come in, sit at her table, watch her eat. She even let her take the dirty dish to the kitchen sink and watched her scrub it clean. Maybe her husband was right. She was not normal. Not a normal wife.

Now she is not a wife at all. She is a business manager. When she returns to the flat, the city's static is clinging to her hair and her eyes ache from the 39-38-37 traffic countdown. The first thing she does is turn on the old TV. It comes on with a faint groan. She showers, drinks a bottle of water from the fridge, cooks, eats, all the while listening to the tribulations of strangers. Actors acting out marriages, divorces, plotting against in-laws, poisoning ears.

After dinner, she sits on the sofa, chin propped up on her knuckles, an elbow digging into her left knee. She nods off sometimes. Like Security downstairs. He falls asleep on that hard, backless stool. Others want him fired because he sleeps, but they forget that the last fellow was much bolder. He not only fell asleep while he was supposed to be on duty but also asked for a monthly supply of mosquito repellent. The building society members had marvelled at the audacity of the request. *The mosquitos keep him awake at least, otherwise he's useless to us.* Before they could fire him, he had quit. Vanished actually. Just disappeared one night and was never seen again. She heard—again, from the sixteenth-floor woman—that the man did not even return to collect the salary owed him.

Where do they go, these men? Back to their village? Or just to the next building, to another security firm? She too needs to go somewhere new. Soon. In fact, why not today? It's Sunday tomorrow. The city is crammed with things to do. Dance classes. Clubs. Women go out, drink. It's legal. Not just girls. Big women with real thighs and grey hair. She's seen some of them, now that she has a car. She drives past clubs and sees them standing outside, smoking on the pavement. There have been moments when she was tempted to stop the car and say something mad. Like, excuse me, but your eyes are so shiny, shinier than the traffic lights. She could go out tonight and stay out as long as she wants. There is no old woman waiting at home with a critical eye on the clock.

On impulse, she steps out today, but she does not put on an evening dress or make-up. She does not take her car either. Instead, she puts on walking shoes and trackpants, and a tiny sling purse the size of her palm with nothing in it except the house keys.

Security is in his usual place, on his backless stool, face turned upward. His finger moves in the air, as if he were counting. She knows how far he will count. Sixteen. It's the highest building in this area. Security does not recognize her at first. He is frowning in concentration when she walks past. In any case, his task is to stave off the dangers that press in. He cannot prevent residents from leaving the building and stepping out into whatever dangers they choose.

She has rarely walked further than the cluster of vegetable carts standing at the far end of the lane. The vendors have packed up and left for the night. At the end of the lane, she pauses. She does not know where the different roads lead from here but there is not much to choose between right and left. She puts one foot in front of the other, and for one hour and twenty minutes, she keeps her eyes fixed on the ground.

A torn red chequered bra with black straps. A

dusty grey shape that turned out to be the carcass of a rat squashed flat by a set of wheels. A yellow-green glob of spit with a fly spinning mad circles around it. A man with an unlit cigarette clamped between his fingers, twanging his nose over and over, as if it were a musical instrument.

A sandal. It is in good shape. Probably fell off a woman's foot. How? It must be the motorcyclists. They ride the bikes right onto the pavements. One of the women riding pillion must have dropped it. Or perhaps a bike rammed into a pedestrian. It's a pretty sandal. Delicate. She has a similar pair that she bought the week after she found the job. Her first job ever. She had never attended any job interviews before she got married but, thankfully, she did finish the management degree, sitting for the final exams weeks before the wedding. This new job didn't fetch her what she might have made if she had been a fresh graduate recruited on campus, but it certainly got her enough to justify a new wardrobe.

Her fancy sandals had cost one thousand and sixty rupees after discount. On the same shopping trip, she had bought a dark-red shade of lipstick, two ready-made cotton suits that hugged her bulk from shoulder to knee, a wine-red plastic hair clutch to hold up a knot of twisted hair above her neck, a batch of golden safety pins tinier than a fingernail, and a set of six hankies. She has not needed the safety pins so far but all the women in office carry a few pins in their purse, or let them hang off glass bangles. She does the same. Safety pins are for safety, after all. For days when something goes wrong.

She walks until the urge to walk leaves her, and then she walks back. At the building gates, she sees him and recognizes him at once even though she has not seen him in years. It's the man from the sixteenth floor. It has been over a year since the incident. She did not go up to his flat to offer condolences despite having read about a condolence meet on the noticeboard near the elevator. Then, she stopped seeing his kids on their way out to catch the school bus.

She had assumed that he had sold the apartment and moved to another part of town. But why would he? Houses are not easy to come by in this city. And she should talk! Just look at her, staying on, even though she doesn't own the flat and despite all the ugly things that were said and done in the house.

She slows down, watching that woman's husband as he stares at the balloon man and the child in a pram. She looks at her watch. It is too late for someone to be out begging. The balloon man is asking for flour. *Wheat flour.*

In a moment, she thinks, he will dip into his wallet. His hand moves to his trouser pocket but he hesitates. She hears him ask, *Where is your woman?*

Whose woman? She takes a step forward, then a step backward. It is not her place to interfere. She hears the reply. *Dead. Gone.* Over the man's shoulder, she sees that Security has reached the gate. He catches her eye and she looks away quickly. The balloon man has noticed her too. He casts glances in every direction, nervous about his growing audience. There's no knowing how these things will turn out. She speaks up then, a notch too loud. *Too late to go home and cook, is it not?*

The balloon man blinks at her. He opens his mouth and closes it. She thinks he will repeat himself, the way beggars do, saying that the child hasn't eaten and how God will bless you for your generosity. But he says nothing after all. He simply looks at her, then looks away.

The man from the sixteenth floor has turned around and she senses that he is feeling like a fool for wanting to be kind. He does not want to be made a fool of. She wants to tell him, don't bother. It's probably a racket. Instead, she says, *Let's just give him a bit of flour and let him go.*

He is squinting, trying to place her. There is little reason for him to remember her. The only time they saw much of each other was that year when they were walking. Round and round and round the building, never stepping outside the gates. She had walked alone. He used to walk with his wife, their first kid in a pram. She walked clockwise, they walked anti-clockwise. Perhaps he had nodded at her. His wife had smiled, her gums showing. Every circle and crossing, that gummy smile. No words were ever exchanged. A bob of the head, now and then.

She goes through the gates, starts to walk ahead, then stops and introduces herself. *I'm from the tenth floor.*

There's no recognition on his face, but he nods stiffly. How much does he know? Not much, she guesses. His wife had had gossip on everyone else though. She would have told him all about the woman from the tenth floor, the one who walks alone even though she has a husband. *No pram to push. Slobby overall. Forever trying to lose weight. Doesn't work out. Nasty mother-in-law.*

Yes, his wife has told him. She can tell, for remembering has brought a visible flush to his face.

Perhaps he wishes that she had not spoken to him, but it is too late now. He tells the balloon man to wait here until he returns. By the time he catches up with her, she is in the foyer, waiting for the elevator and staring down at her shoes. He remembers that his own wife had obstinately refused to wear walking shoes on their evening perambulations around the building. But a year later, he'd found a better paying job that added two hours to his commute, and the walks had ceased. How long ago was that? Six years.

In the elevator, he presses sixteen and, after hesitating for a second, he presses ten. The silence is a loud hum. There must be a reason, she thinks, that she stepped out for a walk tonight. She has not gone out for a walk in years. There must be a reason she returned at this late hour, just when a balloon man pushing a pram happened to meet the husband of that woman. Even in the worst soap operas, nothing happens without cause. The plot is driven by coincidence. Something happens, then something else happens, and there are some consequences based on what the characters do.

When the elevator doors open at the tenth floor, she says, *I have a new bag of flour at home. It is not open yet.*

He says nothing. She steps out of the elevator, then puts an arm against the door. *Will you take it down for me, please? Let this be added to the list of my good deeds in this world.*

She unlocks her flat and goes straight into the kitchen. She has left the front door wide open but he has not stepped inside. She returns with the bag of flour and blinks in surprise. She is about to ask why he is still standing outside the door but decides against it. She gives him the bag in silence and watches him go towards the elevator. Then she goes to the fridge, takes out a cold bottle of water and takes a gulp.

She has not cooked dinner tonight but there are the sweet pooris she bought last week and masala bhakri. It goes well with a cup of tea.

She fills a saucepan with water, places it on the stove, but does not light it. She breathes slowly. Ten minutes pass, or perhaps it is only seven minutes. She stands in the kitchen and breathes slowly, evenly, forcing her heart to beat normally. The doorbell rings at last and she measures out another cup of water, adds it to the saucepan, and lights the stove before answering the door.

The man from the sixteenth floor stands at the threshold. For a few seconds, he says nothing. Then,

Thank you. She does not say, you're welcome, as she should. He starts to turn away. She says, *There's tea on the stove. It's almost done.*

Later, sitting on her old sofa, he begins to tell her about another dead woman, a former colleague's wife. Hit by a train. She and both the kids. He went to their prayer meeting. Decent flat, but the hall was not big enough for so many visitors. Some of the mourners were edged out of the living room and into the kitchen. Some went to sit in the bedroom where the grandparents slept. He was standing in a corner of the bedroom when he overheard a female relative describe how the police had asked the family all sorts of impolite questions. *Where was the deceased going that day? Why was she wearing such a nice sari? She was going to visit a family member obviously. Where else would a woman go with two small children?*

The women in the room had spoken in hushed voices, he said. For a while, they went on about the sari. Abstract geometrical patterns of orange, blue, and green, with a single line of gold thread running along the edge. Not a cheap sari, even the cops could see that. They weren't sure whether it was chiffon or georgette. Someone else said it was semi-silk. That word had become lodged deep inside his head. Semi-silk. He had never heard the word before.

The odd thing was, on that dead woman's body, whatever they could salvage of it, they didn't find any jewellery except for her green glass bangles. *Not even a silver toe ring. Now that's funny, right? A woman who puts on a nice sari usually also puts on a bit of jewellery, doesn't she? And what happened to the gold mangalsutra? She was not the sort of woman who'd remove a symbol of her marriage, not when she was stepping out.*

It could be that the railway police had been lax in their duties. Maybe someone took the toe rings before they got to the body. Who knows who took away the jewellery? Nobody in the family wanted to bring it up, after the way the police had been asking questions. *Who saw her leave the house? Can you take an oath that she was definitely wearing a gold chain when she left? Do you know the contents of her purse? Do you know what we found in her purse?*

Nobody said whether anything special was actually found in that woman's purse. It was strange though, that she didn't wear jewellery that day. *They don't usually take off toe rings, married women, do they?*

He pauses to takes a gulp of tea. It is surely cold by now. She can tell that he wants her to say something about married women, why they do what they do.

Annie Zaidi

He wants her to tell him that the woman who was cut down on the tracks by a train had been merely stupid. Careless, for not using the railway bridge, rather than desperate. She nudges the plate of sweet pooris towards him. He picks one up, bites in. She watches him chew and swallow. He finishes a whole poori before he speaks again. *There was a vase my wife had bought, just a week before the...* he hesitates. *Incident.* He repeats the word. *Incident.*

It was a light metallic vase with a picture of one of the gods painted on it, black and gold tinsel all over. She'd bought it on impulse and regretted it later. It did not suit their home decor. She was always buying things on impulse. Nothing matched anything. Their flat was crammed with trinkets. Useless junk. A cheap metallic vase with a picture of God. It's lying there, upstairs. He can't throw it into the dustbin because of God's image. He never chided his wife though. He never told her not to shop so much. Never told her not to go out with her girlfriends. Late nights. Kitty parties. There was nothing he had ever denied her.

He is looking up at her now. There is a challenge in his eyes, in the thrust of his jaw. She picks up a sweet poori, takes a deliberate bite, and chews for a while before she says, *Your wife was not my friend.*

He blinks. He does not know anyone in this building who does not lay claim to having been his wife's friend. He rubs his fingertips, oily from holding the poori, and makes a gesture as if to get up and go, but then he stays put.

She tells him then, starting with the night his wife brought down a plate of food. *After he left, my husband never called me. He told another woman that his mother was dead. And that other woman, your wife, she came down to tell me. She brought me dinner. Sat over there and asked me to eat. I ate.*

The silence stretches out between them. It is long but not heavy. Finally, she asks if his children are in bed. He says, *They must be.* He doesn't know. They live with his parents now and he visits on weekends. She nods, shrugs.

Much later, after she has taken a warm shower, she steps out into the balcony. A spider's web of yellow light gathers and collapses in the distance. She thinks about the red chequered bra and the circumstances that led to it being out on the street. She chuckles to herself. Who buys red chequered bras anyway? Who has that taste? Now that's not a story she can hope to watch on TV. She remembers the dead rat too and thinks to herself that when a rat is run over, some other rat must grieve.

Annie Zaidi

She will not sleep tonight, she decides, and begins to cook. She doesn't yet know what she's cooking. Something a little more elaborate than her usual dal-rice. She has not cooked a full meal in a long time, living off instant noodles and fried snacks. Ordering lunch at work from a dozen cheap restaurants. She even lets the office girl order in for her. But what a foolish way to live! How little she has learnt from the soap operas. Everyday decisions of what to eat, what to wear, whom to confide in, whom to guard against—this is life. Now look what's happened. She had a visitor today and she could offer him nothing except two sweet pooris bought at the supermarket.

He might come again. Or he might not. He lives upstairs anyway. Tomorrow, she will take a dish upstairs. It is Sunday and he is unlikely to leave the house before lunch. He can eat it if he wants to. Or he can leave it. But he will eat it, she thinks. While leaving, he said, *See you*. Not good night. Not goodbye. See you is what he said, and he seems to be a man of his word.

Acknowledgements

Cities are organisms of which trains, buses, and ferries are the veins and arteries and nerves. I know what I know about any large city only because of affordable, often subsidized, public transport. My gratitude to those who planned, built, conducted, drove, fought for, and repaired these giant systems. I owe you each page of this book.

I am deeply indebted to Musharraf Farooqi, for his close reading, suggestions, and for conversations that helped me knock the manuscript into better shape.

David, Pujitha, and the rest of the team at Aleph—thank you for all you've done with this book, and the ones before.

As always, I owe a debt of gratitude to my immediate and extended families and friends, who have, at various times, in various cities, given me food, shelter, and affection.

Annie Zaidi